THE GARDENER'S WIFE'S MISTRESS

THE GARDENER'S WIFE'S MISTRESS

TYPE EIGHTEEN
BOOKS

Cassondra Windwalker

Library of Congress Cataloging-in-Publication Data

Names: Windwalker, Cassondra, 1974–, author.
Title: The Gardener's Wife's Mistress / Cassondra Windwalker.
Description: 224 pages. – First edition. | Laguna Hills, California: Type Eighteen Books, 2026.
Summary: "When Hayden Hill finds himself suddenly a widower, he struggles with grief, guilt, and the discovery of a shocking secret. He meets his wife's secret connections and becomes involved helping local homeless teens who have been cast out for choosing to be who they are. Rocked by this complicated facet of Shelly's life, he begins to question their marriage, her identity, his past choices, and whether anything he believed about his wife was ever true."—Provided by publisher.
Identifiers: LCCN 2025940196 | ISBN: 9798998947742 (paperback) | ISBN: 9798998947759 (ebook)
LC record available at https://lccn.loc.gov/2025940196

Published by Type Eighteen Books
www.typeeighteenbooks.com

Printed in the United States

for Buttercup and Wolfecub,
and everyone whose soul
is greater than the sum of their parts
(that's you)

CHAPTER 1

Tiny tributaries of mud trickled down the shower walls where Hayden Hill's hands rested on the tile. Hot water sluiced over his bent head.

Deep in a dank, Madagascar forest, oceans and continents away, a ghost orchid grew dreaming under heaps of decaying leaf litter. It would never see the sun. A tiny, star-shaped bloom would emerge for a single day to tempt ants to play pollinators. A vast community of fungal friends would lend all the nutrients it needed to survive.

Hayden thought of Shelly, of her ashes mingled with the rich, dark earth in the backyard, where a young oak tree now stood naked and impudent. His own hands had dug the bed for the sapling's roots, and still, its gawky adolescence felt like an affront to Hayden's dead wife. Not that she had reached an advanced age herself. Who could have anticipated a thunderclap stroke at barely forty-six?

He'd thought the oak was a fine choice for a headstone. Oak trees were repositories of abundant life, playing host to dozens of species in their spreading branches. Symbols of wisdom and storied the lore of numerous languages, the acorn-givers were gatekeepers of all planes of existence. This one might stand for hundreds of years. After a few summers, he could build a bench in its shade, a place to sit and talk with Shelly as he hadn't done enough before she left.

Once he'd heaped the aerated soil around the root ball and looked up at the thin branches, he'd been suffused with rage. Stupid, irrational fury at the woody creature for standing there without any fear, any sense of the time spilling from the tips of its limbs. For slowly, steadily going about its growing business untroubled by the detritus of a too-short life now churned into the soil to feed its roots. Shelly might as well have been a moth felled by the cold, autumnal night air, or a baby bird who left the nest too early, its feathers unready for the wind.

No. Shelly was nothing like broken wings. She was the ghost orchid. Out of sight, her new existence unknown by all who walked above, the processes of her new becoming obscured from his understanding, but certain and sure, nonetheless. Hayden thought of forest giants, prostrated a hundred years ago or more, whose ancient bodies continued as homes and sustenance and carbon-sinks, their essence a perpetual and indelible part of their biome. Shelly's incarnation had shifted form, but she remained, didn't she?

He swore under his breath and shut off the water. He'd forgotten to close the bathroom door, and the air was bracingly cold as he stepped out of the shower. He welcomed the discomfort, toweling himself roughly. Why was he trying to spin platitudes for himself? If they weren't comforting or believable coming from other people, they sure as hell weren't consoling coming from himself.

Shelly wasn't becoming. She wasn't some ineffable presence surrounding him. She wasn't anything but dead.

Hayden didn't bother with pants. A pair of underwear and a threadbare tee shirt would do. He wasn't going anywhere. The parade of well-wishers knocking on his door with casserole dishes and bouquets of flowers had mercifully slowed to a trickle. If anyone showed up, he wouldn't bother answering the door.

He wondered how many people were conscious of the cruel irony of cut flowers as a sop for the bereaved. Maybe bouquets were remnants of a more practical age, a time when people recognized death for what it was and weren't so inclined to avoid looking it in the eye. Sure, people of the past were more steeped in superstitions, but they were more familiar with death, too. History had never held a lot of fascination for Hayden, but he had the idea that prior to the 19th century, virtually every family had buried at least one child and sometimes, several. Half a century was a good lifespan for the ungreedy. And when the time for goodbyes came, it wasn't rushed in a ritual of tinny, piped music and pancake makeup. Families sat with their dead in the house, while friends milled about, sharing bread, drinking beer, and telling stories. There was nothing sanitary about death, and nobody pretended there was.

Back then, cut flowers were part of the dressing of the day. A thoroughly appropriate nod to both the brevity and the beauty of life, and a grimly pragmatic solution to the unavoidable byproducts of decomposition. By the time the blooms drooped, their heady fragrance was no longer able to counter the corpse's stench, and it was time for both to be buried.

But now? The stiff stems and artificially brilliant hues felt like a last revolt against the inevitable, a pointless little rebellion the bereaved were left alone to watch fail. After friends and family, coworkers and acquaintances offered their sympathies and fled as hastily as they could, the house was cluttered with expensive bouquets in various stages of decay. Hayden didn't bother to add water to the vases, to delay the inescapable. Dried petals and leaves and crumbling stamen littered the carpet. This morning, he filled the garbage can with the macabre displays, vases and all.

He didn't need to be reminded that everything sweet and beautiful turned to dust in the end.

Shelly's parents loaded their car with several bouquets after the memorial. Roger and Diane had been as stunned as he, still in shock by the time they had to endure the modern pageantry of death. Hayden wondered if Roger and Diane felt differently about the flowers when they started dying, a grim echo of losing Shelly.

None of them had seen death stalking Shelly's veins. On her last morning, he'd looked into her eyes and hadn't seen any hint of darkness. Hadn't he? Panic swamped him, and he froze, standing at the kitchen counter with a glass in his hand. Frantically, he tried to remember. She'd been making her coffee to take to work as he was on his way out. Maybe their hugs and kisses had become perfunctory, but they never missed a day. She'd been distracted, but then, so had he. He recalled that last kiss, his hands on her shoulders.

She had brown sugar on her lips from the English muffin. He laughed and said something trite about how sweet she was. And her eyes had met his—hadn't they? *Goddammit.* Try as he might, he couldn't picture them. He could see the curve of her cheekbone, her long fingers on the handle of the spoon as she stirred the sugar and cream into her coffee. The purple V of her blouse over her breasts.

Had he not looked into her eyes? Why couldn't he remember?

With shaking hands, he poured out the water in his glass and replaced it with tequila. His little brother Lorne hadn't known how to help, but at least he hadn't pretended otherwise. He simply showed up with copious amounts of alcohol and filled Hayden's cabinets and refrigerator. Lorne's wife Jaciee left the brothers alone after a quick, hard hug. That first night, Lorne stayed over and said almost nothing while his brother sobbed and howled.

Hayden hadn't known he could make those noises. Hadn't known grief would come like physical agony that spasmed all his muscles and wrenched his bones.

Lorne had sat there in the dark, drinking steadily and holding onto his brother when Hayden would let him, retreating to the couch when he wouldn't. Hayden hadn't had a drop of alcohol that night or the next. But tonight—tonight he was grateful for every bottle Lorne had supplied. He'd even brought a bag of limes, lemons, and oranges.

Hayden sliced up a lime, grabbed the saltshaker, and walked into the living room. He realized he should probably eat something, but he wasn't hungry. He pushed aside the blankets and pillows heaped in the recliner and added his glass to the collection on the end table. He hadn't slept in their bed. He didn't know if he ever would again. Maybe he would sleep in the living room from now on.

The first, long sip of tequila was oddly comforting. He had expected it to taste different, somehow. Everything else in the world was different now. But it tasted exactly like tequila. A weird place to find continuity, he supposed, but nothing and everything was weird these days.

He wondered if Roger and Diane were finding comfort in one another, or if they were islanded in separate rooms, trying to find their way alone. People said losing a child was the worst type of grief, but Hayden couldn't imagine anything worse than this. Was it easier if the child was an adult? Or was it worse, the loss heightened by shock? Parents must fear their children dying all the time while they're young, but at some point, maybe they move beyond those anxieties. Once children are grown and settled, they thought they could relax into their old age—but then a thief stole it all away.

He takes another burning swallow. Funny, how an event that stripped people of all artifices brought so many lies in its wake. Dignity, grace, even simple cohesion: all these vanished with that last breath. Death was so terribly slack. Empty. The face, the body, he'd loved so well becoming a thing in an instant. Her hand, just a collection of bones. What had happened to her hand that held his? Where had that gone?

Maybe that was why the lies came tripping in so fast. The truth was too awful and bare. For Shelly's parents, their Methodist religion had always been the scantest of polite veneers, more of a social exchange than anything else. A convenient conduit for their food pantry offerings, and a place to go on Christmas Eve. Couples to invite for game nights. But on the day of the memorial, Diane kept up a running patter about her angel watching over us from Heaven now, about the mystery of God's will, and about how her daughter was with Diane's own mother. Hayden didn't know if Diane believed all that, or if it was just a desperate act of self-soothing. Roger hadn't spoken at all, only stared as tears ran down his cheeks.

Salt, tequila, lime. Hayden pushed himself up and shuffled back into the kitchen. No point in pouring a new glass, was there? He was the only one here. He grabbed the bottle and returned to the chair, pulling the blankets over his bare legs. It was getting cold at night, but he didn't have the will to turn on the heater.

He probably wasn't being any more honest than Diane. What was the difference between claiming your daughter was an angel in heaven and claiming your wife was part of an oak tree that might lend its essence to the cycle of life? Both were attempts to distract from the simple reality: Shelly was gone.

Shelly was gone. Nothing he could do, nothing he could drink, would lessen the severity of that. Wearily, he set the tequila bottle on the table and pushed back the recliner, flipping up the footstool. He stared at the embossed ceiling tiles. He wished he could keep drinking long enough to pull sleep over his eyelids, but the idea of one more swallow nauseated him.

Why hadn't he talked to her more? Even when loneliness tugged at him, even when he'd wonder what was hidden behind her cooling gaze, he'd been secretly relieved at the ease of their familiarity. Their relationship required so little of him these days. They still made love every two or three weeks, and it was good. Every time, he thought they should do it more often. Wrapped in the damp cocoon of her arms, sated with pleasure, he felt closer to her than he felt to himself. But the next day, initiating that closeness would seem like too much effort. There was work to do. The garden to keep up. Their shows to watch. And she was always running errands in the evening, meeting friends here and there.

Autumn was halfway over, and they'd never made it to the river while it was warm. They used to go all the time. When they first married, they'd go with friends. But somehow, they'd lost almost all their couple friends over the years. It wasn't a mystery, he supposed. All their friends had children and changed into moms and dads, while Hayden and Shelly had gone on perfectly content with each other.

At first, they'd been blissfully, deliriously happy. They'd gotten drunk on each other and stayed that way for a long time; Hayden couldn't be sure when or how their relationship had changed.

Shelly had always been driven. No doubt, that was part of what drew him to her. Passion and energy beamed from her mobile face, coiled in ropes around the lithe limbs that seemed frustrated in stillness. She'd been a lush, wild English garden unapologetically juxtaposed against the concrete dreariness of the trailer park life he'd clawed his way out of. So deeply alive, there was nothing of a succulent about her; she stored nothing and absorbed everything. Even her thick masses of brown hair had a life of their own, much to her dismay.

She approached everything in her life with the same verve and focus. The success of her career had less to do with ambition and more to do with how much she absolutely loved her job. Hayden smiled, the curve of his lips prompting an actual ache, remembering how terrifying and heady at once that focus had been when first directed at him.

Shelly had been a financial advisor—for her, the perfect coalescence of science and chaos. She loved math, loved the surety and predictability of numbers, and she had an innate gift for equations. With sparks in her eyes, she'd tell him how the whole universe was a mathematical proposition of beautiful patterns. An inveterate gambler with what he'd thought an unbreakable lucky streak, she loved winning and had no fear of losing. There was always another day, another line to the problem.

Only now there wasn't.

And they'd never made it to the river this summer. Their last summer. Why hadn't he insisted they go? Hayden tried and failed to remember any weekend from June, July, or August. They could have found the time. Nothing more important had happened.

Last year, they'd gone the first weekend after school started so they could have most of the riverbank to themselves. He could see her profile now, her face uplifted to the sun under a ridiculous floppy hat, the reflection of the rushing water spangling over her bare legs. Her blue bikini. Her chipped nail polish. Her upturned nose and the secret smile on her lips.

Her eyes were closed against the light. Why couldn't he see her eyes? Hayden gripped the arms of the recliner, making no effort to staunch his tears. Breathing was a hard enough process to maintain.

Maybe that was the real reason they hadn't gone back this summer.

There'd been something, a shadow or distance between them on that last river trip. He could lie to himself. He wanted to. He could pretend it had been as idyllic as all their other trips. Certainly, nothing had gone wrong—no fights, no unpleasantness.

But there was a stillness. The parts of Shelly that had always flowed into him without boundaries or barriers were now held quiet and motionless behind a wall he couldn't see through. A wall he might have built himself, stone by stone, without realizing it. Every time he kept reading his book when he felt words straining against her lips, every time he headed out to spend the day in the garden instead of wandering with her. Every time he allowed her to retreat into a place he didn't want to go, while the television droned between them. And there, at the river, at the place they'd always come to slough off the rest of the world and turn entirely into each other, Hayden couldn't deny her waters had taken another direction entirely.

He could have dug out a trench between them. But when they came back home, they fell into their regular habits. He didn't mind the demanding work of trench-digging. A gardener liked to get his hands dirty. But he'd been afraid of what lay in her waters and what might happen when they crashed back together. Why risk conflict and ugliness and hard truths when they were so peaceful? Hayden couldn't remember the last time they'd had a fight.

Any mention of the river this summer had been half-hearted and easily dissuaded. Neither of them had wanted to be alone with the other, with only the river and the wind and the trees for distractions. And now alone was all he would ever be.

Regret smelled like limes and liquor. At least he wouldn't be hungover tomorrow; he lacked the energy to get drunk enough for that. Somehow, in the morning he had to drag himself into a full set of clothes and get to the lawyer's office to discuss Shelly's will. She'd been adamant about that sort of thing, all the details he'd never bothered to learn.

Hayden started counting the curlicues in the embossed tiles overhead. Maybe if he counted them all, he'd fall asleep eventually. Maybe not.

CHAPTER 2

Hayden stared uncomprehendingly across the gleaming walnut desk at Jane McGavin. The lawyer looked back at him, patience and compassion writ large on her face. Hayden realized his mouth was agape and snapped his jaw shut.

Jane smiled, rose to her feet, and crossed the room to pour a glass of lemon water from a pitcher that stood on a small table beside a platter of muffins and fresh fruit. "Here. Details like these are a lot to absorb on top of everything else."

Everything else. The euphemisms for death were endless. Hayden clutched the glass of water like a lifeline. The liquid was cool and tart as it slid down his throat. He rallied.

Most of the details weren't much to absorb at all. He and Shelly either co-owned or had one another listed as beneficiaries on all their accounts and property. There was some work to be done, of course: filing with life insurance and getting the death certificate to banks and investment accounts. Jane would handle that. Shelly wanted her jewelry sold and the proceeds donated to a handful of charities she'd listed. Hayden would do that. Somehow. Eventually.

No, none of that came as a surprise. But—

"Rachel's Blooming Bouquets?" he repeated.

"It's a florist shop," Jane said. "Shelly has been a co-owner for about two years. What you do now is entirely up to you, of course, but her wish was that you continue to hold part-ownership rather than selling your share. Even so, I reviewed their contract, and if you should decide to sell, there's a standard clause allowing the partner, Rachel Lundgren, the opportunity to buy you out at a fair market value." Jane spoke briskly, her features carefully smoothed except for a single furrow niggling between her brows.

Hayden felt a matching furrow form on his own forehead.

"Shelly owned a flower shop?"

"Yes."

"But I've never even heard of it."

"Shelly was a prolific and practiced investor. You probably haven't heard of most of the mutual funds you're invested in or stocks you hold, either."

Hayden raised his eyebrows.

Jane flushed. "I admit, one local boutique investment does stand out among the rest of her portfolio, but I'm sure there's a simple explanation. Could Rachel be an acquaintance from school or some other social circle? I'm afraid I was only involved to the extent of completing paperwork."

Hayden downed the rest of the water. "Not any acquaintance I know of. It's strange she never mentioned it. She managed our financial affairs, sure, but we always discussed things—what percentage to invest long-term or short-term, or other assets. I can't believe she became a business owner and never said a word."

Jane's smile was tight, a clean line like the ones Shelly had signed.

He set the glass down on a coaster and leaned forward. "What more do you need from me?"

There were signatures on a blur of papers and a smattering of details Hayden forgot as soon as he heard them. Ever since Shelly died, he'd felt like a child. All the things he thought he under-stood and controlled had been taken out of his hands, while strangers shuffled him from one task to another. First, the doctors, then the funeral directors, then family and neighbors and friends. And now, the lawyer. He'd met Jane McGavin before, brief appointments to deal with dry legalities Shelly thought necessary, but he'd never considered how one day, she'd be a gatekeeper to a road he didn't want to be on, pushing him through into the unknown and locking the latch behind him so there was no chance of return.

Apparently, beyond death lay a well-traveled track with ruts the bereaved were routinely shuttled along; anyone who'd found themselves on the road before knew the way. All he had to do was follow directions. As far as he could see, only the singular path traversed the wasted earth, so how could he feel so lost?

When he arrived back home, he realized he'd reached the end of that road. All the necessaries were over. Modern ritual was horrifyingly brief. Eight days ago, he opened the same front door and smelled a hot curry bubbling away in the slow cooker. He heard Shelly calling his name from down the hall and saw her shoes beside his by the front door. In the bathroom, a damp towel smelled of her pomegranate shampoo.

Eight days ago. Now, not only was she gone, but all the pomp and procedure attesting to her existence was complete. Instead of the deeply furrowed road behind him, an empty field stretched ahead, its masses of waving prairie grasses unmarked by other travelers. From where Hayden stood, not a single tree broke the monotony of the horizon. No winding creek promised secret shade clambering with hidden life. No destination beyond summoned.

And still, into that emptiness was where he was expected to go.

Longingly, he looked back at the path he'd been unwillingly forced along, but even that was gone. Swallowed up in prairie and more prairie. Golden grass waved bleakly in a dull wind that did nothing to lift the oppressive heat. It was almost as if his days spent with Shelly had never been. The endless grim was all there was, all there had ever been, all there would ever be.

Hayden dropped his jacket onto the floor in the entry and went straight to the kitchen. He opened the refrigerator door, and his eyes met a sea of casserole dishes. He grabbed one and stuck it in the microwave.

He unbuttoned his shirt and shed his pants somewhere along the way. When the microwave beeped, he grabbed the meal and a soda before flopping back into his recliner. He barely tasted the food, some combination of pasta, vegetables, and cheese.

Something gnawed at him, something about the lawyer's face. He'd gotten lost in the dusky smoothness of her broad cheekbones, her knobby little chin. Was she older or younger than him? He couldn't tell. He knew, objectively, he'd found her attractive on previous occasions, but today, her features were unfamiliar, almost alien, frightening. Her eyelids blinked mechanically; her cool smile wasn't a smile at all. Was it an apology? For what?

Hayden tried to shift the casserole dish from his lap onto the end table, but the clanking protests of the small army of glasses and plates already occupying the space stopped him. Reluctantly, he gathered the dirty dishes in his arms and deposited them into the kitchen sink.

Hands braced on the counter, Hayden stared dully out the front window. The back yard was his true oasis, but he did love the Japanese willow whose branches framed the kitchen window. A winding, stone pathway led down to the sidewalk he and Shelly would take to downtown pub crawls on balmy summer nights. When had they last done that?

Last April—they'd met some of her coworkers at a craft brewery and had gone gallery to gallery on a First Friday night, an event organized to support local artists. Pleasant enough, but not exactly fun. It had felt more like a professional obligation than an excursion. And before that time—had it been last year? Or even the year before that?

Wasted. He'd wasted so much time. He thought they had years, decades, together. And what did he have to show for the choices he'd made? What had he substituted for time spent with his partner and best friend that could console him now?

He had no idea.

She'd had something of her own, though. A flower shop, of all things. Hayden wasn't sure if this secret felt like an insult or an effort to reach him.

In college, Hayden loved his botany classes. Still, as he was approaching his graduation, there'd been little choice about pursuing further education or finding a way to make a career out of his love of plants.

If he could have earned a doctorate in botany for the sheer pleasure of it, that would have been one thing. But he had no desire to teach, and even less to spend his life in a lab somewhere. At the time, Shelly was doing brilliantly in her career and had already been accepted into a master's program. So, Hayden had parlayed his education into a position with a landscape architecture firm and supported Shelly through the rest of her classes.

Now, he had his own business. He made about a third of what Shelly did, but that had never been a point of contention between them, and his work made him happy. And he thought she was fulfilled with hers, but she must have wanted something more, something different, and never told him.

Why hadn't she told him?

No matter how Jane McGavin tried to spin it, Rachel's Blooming Bouquets didn't feel like an oversight. It felt like a secret.

Hayden turned away from the graceful drooping of the willow's burgundy branches. He pulled the living room curtains closed and returned to his recliner. He pulled the blankets up to his chin and flicked the TV on.

Oh, good. A somebody-murdered-somebody show. He had no idea what time it was, and he didn't care. Tomorrow, he'd go back to work and pretend he was still a real person but tonight, he was done pretending.

How much time had Shelly spent at the shop? Those occasions when he thought she was at the office or out with friends, had she been at the shop, sticking cut stems into Styrofoam? Suddenly, he wished he hadn't tossed the flowers from the memorial service. He could see if any of them had been sent from Rachel's. They were still in the bin in the garage, but there was no question of him summoning the drive to dig them out. He hadn't even managed to move the dishes from the sink to the dishwasher. He'd do that tomorrow, too. Baby steps.

And who cared, anyway? Maybe he'd just throw the dishes away and live off paper plates from now on. Mostly, he wished he never had to eat again. It was such a colossal effort.

Would the florist muddle along just fine without Shelly, or would there be some immediate consequence to her absence? It seemed preposterous to Hayden that, somewhere, someplace, a person he didn't' know could be suffering in the slightest way without his wife. Maybe he could ignore the whole thing, pretend he didn't know the shop existed—until tax time, at least. Presumably, their tax accountant was already well-accustomed to tallying up the numbers from the business. Shelly was nothing if not conscientious when it came to money.

He wondered if this Rachel person had found out about Shelly's death. Hayden didn't think people read obituaries in the paper anymore, even though he'd paid to have the funeral home print a nice one Jaciee had written for them.

Social media. Of course. They'd have found out through social media. Shelly had been active there. He'd even logged on to her account to make the grim announcement after he'd called everyone he could think of. He supposed he could look at her friends and follower lists to see if Rachel Lundgren or the florist shop itself were there. They must be.

Ah. His attention wandered back to the television screen. It was one of those mercy-killing nurses—so predictable. Hayden had a tough time buying the angle of people acting out of mercy. More like a God complex, he thought, trying to hold the power of life and death over the helpless. Maybe it was an attempt at invincibility; if they could choose the date and hour for others, they could fend off the moment when death came for themselves.

But that was nonsense. Chaos always won in the end, and it wasn't even minding the rules of the game.

CHAPTER 3

One of the problems with being a successful business owner was that much of what other people might consider drudgery was delegated out. Although Hayden was out in the field half the time, he also spent many hours in the office, fielding phone calls, scheduling services, running payroll, and reviewing maintenance. He wished he were back at his college job, working full-time during summer as a landscaping grunt for the city. Maybe if he had exhausting, physical labor to fall into when the sun was barely up, he'd be able to still the looping thoughts in his head. Lawnmowers and weed-eaters and leaf-blowers might drown out the roaring silence Shelly's voice had left behind.

He'd *throw himself* into his work; that's what people did, right? But he didn't know how. And phone calls and ledgers didn't hold the promise of mind-numbing exhaustion he craved.

First, he had to survive the initial gauntlet. Every one of his employees had been at the memorial service but still felt they had to make some new acknowledgment or proffer comforting words. He hoped to give off a sense of doing *as well as can be expected*, but he had no idea what that looked like and from the anxious expressions on his employees' faces, he suspected he was missing the mark.

His assistant, Jason, kept dumping out his cold coffee and refilling his cup. Unlike Shelly's complicated, sugary concoctions, Hayden's choice was black. He'd pour cup after cup then forget to drink it.

Again and again, he found himself staring out his office window, with no idea what to do next. Finally, he decided to write out a damn list, bullet-pointing every task, no matter how small. But once they were down in black and white, dread bubbled up from between the lines and suffused the room.

He'd heard people describe grief or trauma as a blur, and he'd never thought to question that. Now, he wondered if the writers were simply uncomfortable with the details to describe them. Desperately, Hayden longed for a blur, but every single instant of the day stood out, sharp as shattered glass. Each moment a prison sentence of its own.

In the afternoon, he shrugged into his jacket like an old man and grabbed his tool bag and gloves. He'd been looking forward to this job, he remembered, although it seemed like that feeling was from another life. They were transforming what had been a cold, concrete space bound by four towering hospital walls into a Japanese water garden.

He thought he could do it. But when he pulled up alongside the company trucks in the hospital parking lot, his hands were shaking. A few days ago, he roared into the lot at breakneck speed, his veins roiling with fear. Shelly's boss had called to tell him she'd collapsed at the office. It took him ten minutes to arrive at the hospital—too long to be able to say goodbye.

The shock hit first. It couldn't be true. Couldn't be real. Shelly was only forty-six. Healthy. Strong. Vibrant. There had to be some kind of mistake. They'd confused his wife with someone else.

Even when he saw her on the hospital bed, still draped in the remnants of their efforts to revive her, his mind couldn't accept it. Uselessly, his hands had framed her face, traced her slack lips. He kissed her cheeks, her empty palms. His eyes searched the cold, quiet room, as if he could urge her spirit to stay.

When a nurse came back, much later, he lay in the narrow bed beside her, his palm resting where her heartbeat should be. They helped him back onto his feet, though he hadn't wanted to leave, and gave him a plastic bag filled with Shelly's things. Kindly but firmly, they suggested he go home, asked if he had someone to help.

Funny how passionate he'd been about the hospital project at first. The concrete patio was a relic of the seventies, a place for smokers in the heart of the complex. Ugly and utilitarian, with concrete benches and cigarette bins, it had been repurposed as a general outdoor area once the hospital had become non-smoking. But it wasn't welcoming. Now the administration wanted to transform it into a space reflective of the peace and healing they wanted their patients and families to experience. Hayden had known exactly what he wanted to do with the area. Picking the right plants would be a challenge because the walls limited sun exposure and vastly increased the heat in the open air. He envisioned a shaded place with bubbling water, willowy, dwarf trees and thick mosses and lichens, flowering mounds and composite benches that simulated the warmth of wood but wouldn't decay. He had designed a meandering path and various water features, so the limited square footage still managed a feeling of boundless wandering. A secret garden. Jason had supplied him with a handful of haikus evoking a sense of tranquility. Donors could add their names beneath the poet's on concrete steppingstones.

People needed a place to sit and absorb the sort of terrible news hospitals so often dispensed. How remote and theoretical this thought had seemed! When Hayden met with the hospital administrator in charge of the project, she walked him around the various wings and took him into the small, interfaith chapel. Hayden shuddered, remembering that room. Cold, beige, and impersonal, its only concession to solace being the dim lighting. Hayden couldn't imagine how that room made anyone feel better.

Maybe grief was different for religious people, but Hayden didn't believe that. There was a reason why soaring cathedral ceilings simulated the branching canopy of the forest, a reason why stained-glass images needed the sun. When people were broken, nature healed. As much as they tried to divorce themselves from it with all their conveniences and constructs, human beings were an integral part of the natural world, and it was to the natural world they turned for restoration.

He'd been so sure of this, although he hadn't yet experienced any great tragedy in his own life. His parents were still alive. His mom flew out from Florida for Shelly's memorial, and his dad called from Arkansas—about as much as Hayden expected where he was concerned. A couple of high school friends had died since graduation, no one close.

Looking at the looming hospital from the safety of his truck, all he wanted was to get back to his chair at home, pull the blankets over his head, and count his breaths till he fell asleep.

Hayden drove back to the office and sat for a while in the parking lot. He didn't want to face Jason's expectant face and explain why he was there instead of on the job. Or he could join one of the other two crews on other jobs.

He could. Couldn't he?

He couldn't. He'd used up every scrap of energy on this little failure.

Grimly, he turned the key to start the engine. He'd try again tomorrow.

The next four days weren't any easier, but Hayden muddled through. He told his project manager he trusted her to implement the plans for the hospital project and to call him if she hit any snags. He split his afternoons between the other two crews. They didn't need him, exactly, but one of the hallmarks of the reputation he'd built was that every job was finished on time or early. In their field, this wasn't something taken for granted. He'd kept his company small by taking only the jobs he really wanted. He managed to support the families of twenty people, give or take, a number that fluctuated based on the season, and made a respectable paycheck for himself. He didn't need more than that.

Most days, he wanted less. But too many people counted on him now to simply check out.

By the end of the week, Hayden felt as if he'd lived through ten years in five days. He was blunt with himself and said the word death often, fiercely, unadornedly. She hadn't passed, or left, or gone on. She'd died. She was dead. He needed to say that, over and over and over, or he wouldn't believe it at all.

Even so, he forgot every time he fell asleep. He longed for the bliss of unconsciousness but dreaded waking. He'd open his eyes and wonder why he was in the recliner in the living room. Had he fallen asleep watching a show with Shelly? Then the realization would crash over him, all new. The pain was so gutting it registered as a physical sensation, but nothing could ease it. He tried to keep his eyes open as long as he could. Even a few moments nodding off came with a terrible cost. Every time he woke, he became a widower all over again.

Concentration was an impossibility. He had a good team at the office, capable and thankfully, patient. Somewhere in the back of his mind he understood that, just because his life didn't matter anymore, their lives needed to continue. He did his best to go through the motions and didn't protest when they took tasks out of his hands or fixed his mistakes.

One thought, one question, kept forcing its way into his dull misery: *What had Shelly been doing with Rachel's Blooming Bouquets?*

By Saturday, the puzzle had worn his mind raw. He couldn't ignore it anymore. He Googled the directions and set out.

He didn't know what he'd been expecting, but he was surprised. The shop was in midtown, the more modern, always-bustling, hustling part of the city where the chain restaurants and shops and newer businesses were located. Rachel's Blooming

Bouquets was in a strip of businesses with bright, contemporary storefronts and shaded with sidewalk trees that would no doubt need to be replaced in a few years when their stunted roots and exhaust-choked leaves finally gave up.

He backed the truck into a space across from the front door and waited until he saw someone else go in. He wasn't sure what he was going to say, or how he'd approach whoever was there. He didn't want attention focused on him as soon as he walked in.

He pulled his ballcap down as he walked through the glass door, wincing at the bell that rang out merrily over his head. He needn't have worried. The clerk or shopkeeper was thoroughly engaged with the man who'd come in before him.

"What kind of flower shop doesn't sell flowers?" the man was asking with a raised voice.

"We do sell flowers," the woman responded.

Both were out of view from where Hayden stood. He was in a broad aisle beside a window display of bonsai trees of assorted sizes placed at random heights. On the other side, large pots of miniature gardens edged with trimmed boxwood overflowing with flowering thyme and sweet alyssum loomed in effusive color.

"But all of ours are living flowers, sold in pots. I'm happy to help you find something your wife would enjoy. Do you know her favorite flower or color?"

"I'm not sure she'd appreciate me bringing home one more thing for her to take care of. I was looking for a dozen roses, not a commitment. I should have gone to the grocery store."

"Probably." The woman's voice was cheerful. "If life with you has her so overwhelmed that watering a plant would be one thing too many, you've probably got bigger problems than finding roses. But good luck!"

A reluctant grin tugged at Hayden's mouth. He scooted farther down the aisle as the woman herded the man toward the door.

"This place is never gonna last. I'm telling everyone what terrible customer service and crap products you have."

"I'm sure that will devastate me," the woman said placidly as the doorbell jangled. "No doubt your friends were my key customer base."

She was chuckling softly as she turned back and started slightly when she saw Hayden. He expected her to plaster a smile on her face and adopt a polite demeanor, but her warm, brown skin went ashen, and her face took on an expression that could only be described as dread.

"Hayden," she said quietly.

"Rachel?" he asked.

"Yes." She wiped her hands on her green, flowered apron, though they looked perfectly clean to Hayden.

"How do you know me?" he asked stupidly, as if that were the most important thing.

She hesitated, choosing her words. "We met at the memorial."

He stared at her, trying and failing to place her in his memory. The mind in trauma is such a tricky, untrustworthy place. Hayden could recall every detail of the horrible moments in the funeral director's office. The price sheets. The color of the thank-you cards. The songs Shelly couldn't hear. The wood grain and satin fabric of the coffin she would lie in only long enough for her corpse to be stared at before she was burned to ash. Picking not one but two urns so she could be gruesomely divided into bits for her husband and her mother.

The memorial service itself, however, was like a forgotten dream. He'd let everyone else do the speaking. Lorne had asked him. "Are you sure you won't be sorry later?"

Hayden was sure. There was no mystery to Shelly, nothing to be revealed. The crowd filling the funeral home was there precisely because they knew Shelly—her warmth, humor, passion, and kindness. They didn't need him to tell them why they should have loved her while she was here. But God, he wished he'd loved her better himself.

He hadn't heard a word anyone said. He sat in the pew staring at the half-moon of Shelly's plaster-painted face rising above the gleaming wood of the expensive casket and willed her to open her eyes, to sit up, to make a miracle of their terribly ordinary life. *Come on, honey. This can't be how it ends.*

After the talking had stopped, he was guided to a corner of the room where everyone filed past him. Rachel must have been one of those people, but he had no memory of her golden-brown gaze, her black braids or square shoulders.

Facing her now in a shop he'd never noticed before today, he wondered how wrong he'd been about Shelly. Maybe there was more to say, more to tell, after all.

CHAPTER 4

Rachel retreated to the counter. Hayden imagined she felt safer, more powerful there. She certainly looked that way, and he lost a shade of confidence.

"Your attorney called," she said.

So far, so good. She already knew about Shelly's death, and she already knew he was the half-owner of this place.

"I don't know what I'm going to do," he said.

Golden fire flared in her brown eyes. "I don't need anything from you. I can manage the shop on my own. All you need to do is stay away and collect the quarterly earnings—when there are any."

The last four words were muttered, but Hayden heard them.

"Is the shop in trouble? Shelly was an excellent business-woman. She'd never be part of a failing venture."

Rachel shook her head. "What a dumb thing to say. Of course, she would. Swooping in on failing businesses was a fundamental part of her job. But Blooming Bouquets wasn't one of them. Every new business struggles the first couple of years. Shelly believed in me, and we are making it. Mostly."

She closed her mouth tightly and set her hands on the counter. Her defensiveness slid off him like oil on water. He didn't have the energy for his own emotions right now, much less anyone else's.

"You said the business is fairly new?"

"Yes." She spoke more slowly now, considering her words. "Almost two years ago."

"You wouldn't have this if it weren't for her."

A long pause. "No. I wouldn't."

Hayden allowed his gaze to drift slowly over the interior. It was much larger than most florists he'd seen, though he couldn't say he'd been to many. They made no sense to him. From his point of view, handing someone an armful of dying flowers cut off from their connection with the rest of the universe implied about as much love and joy as handing someone a box of dog ears or cat tails.

Shelly knew that, of course. She teased him about it often enough, especially around Valentine's Day or their anniversary. Why wouldn't she have told him about Rachel's Blooming Bouquets? Crowed over it, even.

Instrumental folk music played softly overhead. Fragrance and color billowed in the cool, humid air. Trapped in various pots and beds, Hayden could almost hear the plants humming as they drew up water and breathed out oxygen. The shopkeeper might be abrasive, but the shop itself was a place of peace, nothing like the florists he despised, with their refrigerated flower morgues, their bobbing balloons and plastic ribbons.

The door jangled. Rachel glanced at him. Probably worried about what he might say in front of a customer, he thought. But he wasn't looking to make trouble.

Hayden heard a woman caution her children not to touch anything. "We still need to talk." he said.

"Do we? I can send you an annual check. Nothing needs to change."

"Everything has changed," Hayden said. "How about we meet for coffee somewhere? I have a few questions." And I want them answered on neutral ground, he added silently.

Rachel gave a quick nod. "Fine. There's a coffee shop two doors down. I can meet you tomorrow morning before I open. Eight-thirty?"

"I'll see you then."

She moved past him and greeted her new customers so graciously that Hayden wondered if she might have multiple personalities. He slipped out, back into the autumn sunlight. Back in his truck, he stared at the front windows and overhead, the flower-decked lettering with the shop's name. He looked for some trace of his wife, some hidden messages, but he saw nothing familiar at all.

He didn't know what he'd been expecting. Some connection, maybe, some recognition of this person now added to their lives. But Rachel Lundgren was only a stranger. Hayden sighed, deflated. Already, he regretted setting up a meeting with her. He didn't really care about any of the business details, or why Shelly had this thing for herself. As long as it didn't sink and drag him under, it didn't matter to him if Rachel's Blooming Bouquets wrote him a check once a quarter for two cents.

Shelly would have scolded him, insisted he take a practical approach and make a sound, fiscal decision about the place. She would have asked him to maintain some oversight. Or would she? The flower shop didn't compare to any of their other investments; she'd taken a singular stake—and maybe an emotional one? But what was it? Hayden didn't even know how Rachel had met his wife.

Maybe Jane McGavin was right, and the shop was a women-forward charity case of Shelly's, but Hayden didn't buy that. She would have told him, and she wouldn't have taken half-ownership in one venture. Too much risk, and too much commitment for someone with a full-time job. No, something here was personal.

Hayden started the truck and shifted out of the parking lot. There was no point in ruminating endlessly, and by tomorrow morning, he would have all the answers. Maybe Rachel Lundgren would buy him out, and he'd never need to think about it again. But if the shop were barely solvent, she couldn't afford to do that.

When he reached home, he walked to a side gate and into the backyard.

His mind was so dark, it was a struggle to perceive the sunlight shimmering through the many shades of green leaves, but the garden was his haven all the same. Hayden despised lawns and their sterile consumption of resources. The front, much to their neighbors' dismay, was a xeriscape, the rocks and pebbles broken up by clumps of native wildflowers Hayden allowed to riot as they liked. The small willow bent over the kitchen window stood as a dramatic focal point. Just this side of the HOA's requirements, the design was quite lovely, even if it was different from the rest of the postage-stamp-sized, bee-starved lawns on their street.

In the back, where a privacy fence obscured prying eyes, Hayden took full advantage of the region's regular rainfall. Pebbled paths and broad flagstones wandered among trees and flowers, shrubs and grasses. Insects buzzed and hummed, and birds twittered and sang. It still wasn't finished, exactly. Hayden didn't figure a gardener was ever done adding to or adapting their design. Each plant added its own entire family of lifeforms and systems. Out in the wild, plants formed all sorts of strange, deeply interconnected relationships with each other, fungi, insects, mammals, and birds. A suburban yard didn't offer the same commune between flora and fauna, but Hayden liked to imagine they were building a world of their own, all the same.

There were still some rather bare—or at least, untamed— patches. In one of these, Hayden had planted Shelly's oak. Down near the back fence, where the property ran down to a neighborhood pond surrounded by walking trails. His legs shook as he walked to it, placed his hand on its slender trunk. He'd forgotten to eat again, hadn't he? Probably.

Leaves fluttered around him. Soon, they'd turn scarlet. Transformation was the hallmark of all living things—or maybe just material things. Even cliffs and canyon walls changed, worn away by the same time that wore away channels of age in his skin and blurred his vision when he tried to read at night.

Had Shelly transformed? Did she go on at all? Hayden didn't know. Still somewhat influenced by the casual religious adherence of her parents, Shelly had believed in a benevolent, creative force into which all life ultimately flowed. She was as comfortable calling it God as she was calling it the Universe. Hayden, whose childhood had been devoid of all philosophy besides survival, was much nearer to atheism. Even that seemed too devout a description for what he believed or didn't. The question was uncomfortable, and until now, he'd avoided it without much deftness required. Understanding life as it was, and as it had been, was quite fascinating enough for him.

But now, the notion of Shelly completely gone was too awful to contemplate. Maybe some people would accuse him of a soft intellect, or claim he wanted to be appeased by a comfortable lie rather than face a hard truth. But this was a simplification as shallow as his previous soullessness.

He wanted to believe nothing of her bright spirit remained, but he couldn't. Shelly had taken up too much space in the world. When a beech tree fell, it was not gone. It still occupied the world. Still fed, sheltered, and evolved. This had to be true for people, too. Didn't it? Hayden didn't know if existence was a singular consciousness that retained its identity, or if Shelly's spirit had joined with the spirits of the mountain columbines and the desert foxes and the evaporating glaciers, if her particular hue had merely deepened the color of the wind at the back of the universe.

But he was sure she still *was*. Somehow. Something. Energy could not be created or destroyed. And there was so much more energy in Shelly than carbon could account for.

His sister-in-law Jaciee had told him not to worry about the rules when it came to navigating his grief, that if something felt soothing or important, it didn't need to make sense. She said he shouldn't feel compelled to explain himself to other people. Jaciee had already lost both parents. He supposed that made her an expert of sorts. Deciding she was right, he cleared his throat and tried out his voice.

"What were you doing with that flower shop, Shelly?" He looked up at the tree. "Why didn't you tell me? What did you see in that unpleasant woman that made you keep her existence secret from me?"

Maybe he was being melodramatic. It didn't feel that way, though. He'd always considered Shelly his partner. Now, he found out she was someone else's partner, too. Someone he didn't even know. And it hurt. Damn it. He hadn't thought he could perceive a new wound, swamped as he was by all this billowing sadness, but it hurt.

He wanted to sink down onto the soft ground under the tree and wait for an answer. But he wasn't sure he'd get up again if he did that. His bones and heart were heavy. He forced himself to get out of bed every day and move, because he understood instinctively his cells were slowing, slowing, slowing. Life was supposed to be an instinctual thing, but his internal processes felt as if they were heading toward extinction.

He contented himself with laying his hand briefly on the young trunk. If he listened closely, he could hear the water and nutrients coursing up against gravity, carrying animus and strength. Sure, he could. He shook his head and walked back up the yard, across the flagstone patio, to the back door. How heavy his feet were.

CHAPTER 5

Apparently, Sunday mornings were slow at the coffee shop. Hayden would have preferred more bustle and hum. He carried his black coffee and a cinnamon roll to a table by the window. Classical music played softly in the background. The baristas were talking and laughing, their conversation rising with the crescendo of the cappuccino machine. A couple sat talking by the electric fireplace. A woman read a novel while stirring her steaming beverage. Not nearly enough activity for Hayden to lose himself in contemplating.

A weird discomfort sat on the back of his neck. It felt strange to be having breakfast out with someone besides Shelly, stranger still with another woman. He was sipping his coffee when Rachel came through the door with a gust of frigid air.

And Rachel Lundgren had something of a tempest about her. Her thick, black hair seemed to snap with electricity, and energy hummed along her defined jawbone. Her eyes scanned the near-empty room and quickly rested on him, their golden-hazel color arresting and clear. She would be downright fierce if it weren't for the freckles dusted faintly over her cheeks.

She came straight over, shrugging out of a long, brown leather jacket and unwinding two scarves from her neck. She draped the whole pile over the chair opposite Hayden.

"So, you did show. Be right back."

Before he could ask why she thought he wouldn't, she was gone. Hayden stared at his cinnamon roll. Normally, he'd eat it with his hand, but he didn't want to be licking frosting off his fingers in front of her. On the other hand, eating with a fork was hopelessly persnickety. Wasn't it? Why did he care what she thought?

He was still debating this when she came back with a cinnamon roll of her own and some creamy, sugary drink Shelly would have loved. She started talking as she slid into the seat.

"You said you had questions. What do you want to know? I can email you access to the books, but it will be read-only. I don't want to risk the figures getting messed up."

She grabbed a fork and started digging into her pastry. That was decided, then. Hayden picked up his fork, too.

"How involved was Shelly?" he asked.

Rachel held her fork aloft; a cinnamon-coated strip hung from the end. "In the business? Her part was more strategic than labor-intensive. She didn't work shifts, but she spent a lot of time there. We planned everything together." Her voice broke, and she dashed at her eyes with the back of her hand.

Hayden hadn't even considered that Shelly's business partner would be grieving. It was hard to wrap his head around the idea of someone he didn't know mourning his wife. Shelly didn't tend to form intense emotional relationships with work colleagues, but nothing about this investment was typical. And it wasn't as if her coworkers had been unaffected. They'd all shown up to the funeral, and many showed emotion. Funerals are sad, though; there was no way of telling if they had suffered real loss. But something about Rachel's tears were intimate. Genuine.

"How did you contact her?"

Rachel blinked slowly. "By phone, most of the time. Email."

"No, I mean how did you approach her for the investment? Did you go to her office, or meet at one of those networking brunches?"

"Oh, no. She was a customer at the florist where I used to work."

Hayden frowned around a bite. "Really? She never brought flowers home."

Her shoulder rose then fell. "Well, she bought a single stem every Monday. To get her through the week, she said. One time she happened to mention how you never bought flowers, that you were a gardener and didn't like cut blooms."

Rachel's voice was matter of fact, but the words cut deep. Regret choked him. What a small thing it would have been, to buy Shelly flowers. She'd never asked for them. He'd always made his own opinions so big and loud; it had never occurred to him that her silence wasn't assent.

"I told her I felt the same way," Rachel said. "How is it an expression of love to give something that is dying? I'd always dreamed of opening a different sort of flower shop, one that sold living blooms."

Startled, Hayden dragged his gaze out of the bottom of his coffee cup to meet Rachel's. "It was your idea?"

Rachel smiled, and little sunbursts of lines appeared beside each eye. "She laughed at me. Said her husband felt the same way, and asked if I meant a nursery? I said no, nurseries are for gardeners. People with yards of dirt and green thumbs. I wanted to specialize in small, beautiful plants that even the organically challenged could keep alive in a small space with minimum effort. Plants you would give for the same occasions, only these wouldn't wither and have to be thrown away in a few days."

"I think that's brilliant," Hayden said. It was like hearing a thought out of his own mind before he had it. Maybe this woman wasn't all bad. She was small and slight but somehow took up a lot of space. That wasn't inherently a bad thing, was it?

"Shelly thought it was crazy, but we kept talking about it. I was more focused on individual customers, but she wanted to think about corporate customers. Keeping plants in the office improves health, morale, and productivity. Eventually, she offered me a partnership."

"Huh." Hayden stacked his empty plate on top of hers. "I'm going to get another cup of coffee. Want more of whatever that is?"

"No, I'm good."

Hayden carried their plates over to the bussing caddy and refilled his cup at the self-service drip coffee station. Rachel's words bounced around his head, and he struggled to hold onto them. He had no reason not to believe her. Still, something was missing. Why wouldn't Shelly have told him about this idea, which almost seemed to have evolved from his own thoughts?

He glanced back at the table. Rachel stared out the window, her shoulders slumped and her chin resting on her hand.

But when he slid back into his chair, her attention snapped back to him. Shoulders straightened, and eyes blazing as bold as ever.

She was an echinopsis, Hayden decided. A hedgehog cactus, covered in prickly spines but dressed in beautiful blooms. He wondered if her waters were as dangerous as the mescaline found in the desert plants. An intoxicant prone to delusions and hallucinations, the sort that could persuade careful, practical Shelly to hand over not only her wallet but her time.

"I'm still confused about why she chose this venture. Shelly dealt with million-dollar accounts every day. She managed our funds, and we did very well. I don't understand why she'd take such a risk, even one she could afford, for basically no return. And I don't understand why she didn't tell me about it."

Rachel's face shuttered. Maybe he had insulted her, but how else could he have said it? She had to know she was minor compared to Shelly's usual investments.

THE GARDENER'S WIFE'S MISTRESS 35

"Look, I can answer questions about the business, but I'm not here to explain your wife to you. Obviously, she had her reasons. And your lawyer told me her will stated she wanted you to keep her share of the business. Are you going to honor her wishes?"

Abrasive, Hayden thought. Resentment flared. Who did she think she was, anyway? Logically, he knew why Jane McGavin would've spoken with her about the disposition of the business, but it felt like an unbearable intrusion. As if Rachel had any right to pass judgment on what he did with his dead wife's assets. Who knew what Shelly had been thinking when she wrote that? This woman didn't need to attach some emotional significance to a business decision.

"I haven't decided," he told her.

"You should know I can't afford to buy you out," she said.

"Shocking." He was the one who'd lost someone. Everyone else walked on eggshells around him these days, but she was throwing glass.

Maybe the shop was all she had, he thought.

He dug for his wallet and fished out a business card. "Here. My email address. Send me the info for the books. Is there anything you need from me while I'm making up my mind? Any responsibilities Shelly had?"

Rachel took the card. "Responsibilities?" she said. "No."

"All right, then. I'll be in touch."

The coffee boost drained away as he walked out. It was only around nine in the morning, and he felt like he'd run a marathon. God, he hated these days. So interminably long. Every hour felt like a year to live through, a blank calendar he didn't want and couldn't escape. Why should he have so much time and Shelly have none? Even the air felt stale; the cold touched his skin but didn't affect him. Everything looked gray, had looked gray for a long time.

Rachel's Blooming Bouquets. There was color at that shop. Effusive. Flamboyant. Maybe the reason Shelly had spent so much time there was as simple as that. But why hadn't she wanted to share that time with him?

He didn't look back, but for some reason, he imagined Rachel slumping over the table again. Maybe sobbing. He couldn't shake the thought.

CHAPTER 6

Grief was a wild rhododendron forest. Tangled, impassable, choking all light from any other sprout attempting to grow. An uninvited, foreign invader claiming every inch of ground as its own. Ebullient with beauty, bringing memories of the lost more dangerous than the darkness lurking under the spreading branches. Hayden wanted to lose himself in those petals, to let the rhododendrons ramble till nothing else remained.

He knew it was pointless, but his mind kept harping on the unfairness of it all. He understood enough about ontogeny and its end to know there was nothing unfair about death: it happened when it happened. An intersection one rarely saw coming, although street signs warned of the ahead.

But death felt unfair. Like cheating, a theft, something he could undo if only he could rework the equation. The math didn't add up.

And still, every time he opened his eyes, the sum was the same.

After he met with Rachel, he received access to the business accounting and emailed it directly to their accountant—his accountant now—without a glance. He'd always left those details to Shelly and the accountant, and there was no reason to change now. He wasn't even sure what he'd wanted to know, or if his request had only been a posture, a way to show Rachel Lundgren he was a person of discernment, someone who knew how to make rational decisions.

Again, why did he care what she thought of him? He wasn't convinced he liked her, but she had been important to Shelly for some reason, and he felt compelled to figure out why.

Hayden didn't like to think about how comfortable and complacent his marriage had become. No—not his marriage. His whole life. How could happiness be a bad thing? He had taken for granted his calm, good life with Shelly. The usual things people fought over—childrearing, money—weren't issues for them. Shelly was practical when it came to finances, and he'd never been one of those men who ranked their success with expensive purchases. He and Shelly had plenty.

They hardly ever fought. Sometimes, they disagreed over stupid things: she was always late, he tracked dirt into the house. But they didn't attack each other. They didn't break each other's hearts.

Could that have been a bad thing? Maybe they didn't fight because they didn't talk about anything important enough to fight over. No. That couldn't be right.

When they were young, before they had more money, they spent their weekends at museums and public gardens. They talked about everything then. Chechnya. The Body Worlds exhibit. The fate of the Kursk crew. Climate change.

Hayden couldn't remember the last time he'd really watched the news. The more time he spent with his plants, the less he cared about politics—not because he didn't think it mattered, but because he doubted the intention of people to change. Conflict had never been his strong suit. One of the things he loved about Shelly was her graciousness. She had an innate ability to put people at ease even as she schooled them about all the ways they were wrong. She'd been the warrior; he'd been content as her shield bearer.

But had he buried her shield somewhere along the way? Try as he might, Hayden couldn't be sure of the last fight his wife had been compelled to take up. Maybe she'd been as complacent as he. Or maybe he'd had no idea what was happening in her life.

In some ways, they'd lived in two separate worlds—wasn't that proof of the healthiness of their relationship? They had their own interests, their own careers, and still found happiness and solace in each other. At least, he had believed they did. But maybe it had devolved to mere habit.

They had a varied set of mutual friends. Didn't they? Now, he realized none of their social circle was from outside their professional worlds. Not one of them would Hayden call in the middle of the night, when he woke up and discovered afresh that Shelly was dead. They were cocktail friends, not whiskey and tears friends.

Except for this Rachel.

No, Hayden corrected himself. She was an investment partner. But hadn't she been a friend first, as they talked over Shelly's Monday flower purchase? Or had his shrewd wife been angling for profit all along? Something new and different.

Hayden didn't want to rewrite their story into a tragedy. He didn't want to second-guess and doubt and recolor every memory in shades of Rachel—or whatever else had created the quiet but undeniable pool of distance between them for some time. He didn't want to lie to himself, either.

There was only one way to find out. Maybe in silly Victorian novels or soap operas, people kept detailed diaries where they recorded their secret longings and motivations, but Shelly had never been inclined to wile away hours thinking about herself. If he wanted to know what Shelly had seen in Rachel and in her shop, he'd need to walk where she walked.

He wouldn't feel guilty about taking time away from work. He'd made several attempts to join his crews out in the field this week but had only been in the way. He'd designed every project, but he couldn't do anything right. The crew averted their eyes, and he knew he was slowing them down.

And in the office—that was the worst. Stuck in a room of his own, with four walls and a screen? Hayden had no idea the number of times Jason had found him staring into space, hopelessly spiraling in sorrow and rage. Poor kid tried his best to cure his boss with coffee and muffins, but there was no denying Hayden's utter uselessness to the business at the moment.

Luckily, this had been one of his and Shelly's many points of agreement: hire people you trust and treat them well, and the business will take care of itself. The only real job of any manager was to support his people. And Hayden was lucky to have great people.

The best thing he could do for them was to get out of their way for a while.

To Rachel's Blooming Bouquets it was, then. Wouldn't Rachel be thrilled? Hayden felt his face stretch into…a smile?

CHAPTER 7

Hayden felt a little silly, slipping into the shop behind another customer again and disappearing down an aisle before he could be greeted. Lurking was becoming one of his talents. Old dogs could learn new tricks, maybe.

An unfamiliar voice asked the customer—an older woman with a purse the size of a small suitcase—how they could help. Not Rachel, then. This voice was pitched deeper, and the syllables rolled more slowly. Hayden peered between the ferns.

The clerk was tall and fair, but hunch-shouldered, as if trying to seem smaller. Pink-tipped curls cascaded over a black Ramones tee shirt, and although Hayden was sure he caught a glimpse of beard scruff, the clerk's features sported elaborate winged eye makeup, glittering lashes, and painted lips that matched the hair. He squinted at the nametag but couldn't make it out.

He jumped a little when the person's questioning eyes met his. "I'll be with you in just a moment."

"Oh, no. That's all right. I'm exploring for now. Take your time helping her."

The old lady looked at him with a crinkled brow.

Hayden turned and devoted his attention to the succulent

gardens planted in long, narrow concrete trenches. This was a stupid idea. No, wait. This was *his* shop, too. Sure, he didn't know the first thing about it, the employees, nothing. But there was only one way to learn. Some discomfort and awkwardness were a small price to pay for understanding what his wife had been doing with her life before it was stolen away.

The clerk finished ringing up a diminutive rose tree for the other customer and came to check on him. "I'm Melodie," she said, smiling and lifting her chin. "Do you see anything you like? Looking for something in particular?"

Hayden stuck out his hand. "I'm Hayden Hill. I'm the part-owner of this shop—at least, I am now."

He tried to say, *Since my wife died and left her ownership to me,* but the words dried up and stuck to the back of his throat. He coughed.

To his surprise, Melodie's eyes filled spontaneously with tears. "You're Shelly's husband?"

Instead of letting go, she clasped his hand more tightly. "I'm so sorry. I loved Shelly. She was a fantastic human being."

Without warning, Hayden felt his face crumple. He closed his eyes, fought for control.

Mercifully, Melodie let go immediately and stepped back, giving him space to breathe. Nobody had told him how a whole lifetime of pent-up tears would lose their levees when his friend and partner died. How all the myths he'd been told and believed about manhood would collapse at the simplest kindness. How his days and nights would be nothing but a ganglion of tears and more tears.

When he opened his eyes, Melodie had turned and was pretending to check the leaves of the plants near them. If possible, she'd curled even more in on herself, as if trying to take up less space. Hayden was sorry his own roots and limbs and leaves were rampaging all over, but he didn't know how to retreat.

"Her service was lovely. So many people showed up," she said quietly.

"You were there?" Hayden hadn't noticed her, like he hadn't noticed Rachel.

"I sat in the back."

"Oh, well, thank you for coming. I was glad the place was so full for her."

"It's weird, isn't it, how someone can hold so much light inside them, and then wink out?" Melodie cleared her throat.

Hayden blinked. Not many people had the courage to be so direct, but it was a relief to hear someone else say aloud the hard truth that consumed him in every hour, waking or sleeping. "Yes," he said hoarsely.

"What can I show you? Do you want a tour?"

Hayden seized on that. Something defined. Something tangible. "Yes. That would be great. I don't know anything about the shop. I'd like to be where she was, do what she was doing, for a while. If I won't be in the way."

"Not at all." Melodie seemed to breathe easier, her chest expanding as she straightened her shoulders and rose to her full height. "So, you already know about the philosophy of Blooming Bouquets and what sets us apart from other flower shops."

"Yes." He cleared his throat. "I'm a gardener myself—more on a corporate level. Landscaping and such."

"Oh, wonderful. Then this will make perfect sense to you. I'm not at all surprised Shelly married a gardener. She was a grower."

Hayden stored the thought away for later—whatever it meant.

Melodie led the way through the aisles, pointing out the organization of the flower types and sizes. Each plant was affixed with a large, clear label identifying how much care would be needed, and there were comments on the historical or literary connotations of the flowers, explaining their traditional symbolism in various cultures.

"Is Rachel working today?" Hayden asked. She was the main person he associated with this secret side of Shelly, and he felt drawn to her, like a scab he ached to pick.

"She'll be in after lunch. She has a greenhouse at her house. It's where we start most of our plants. We split our shifts between the greenhouse and the store, so we don't get burned out with customer service, you know?"

Hayden hadn't worked any sort of retail job, but he'd spent a brief stint in food service in high school; he imagined there were similarities. Even with his landscaping business, the customer interface was usually his least favorite part of the job. There were exceptions, of course, but people tended to view people working in any service capacity as if their only value lay in what could be wrung out of them. Requiring every interaction to be measurable in productivity and efficiency was exhausting, as far as he was concerned.

"I'd much rather have my hands in dirt than banging away on a cash register any day," he said

Her eyes crinkled as she smiled.

Hayden wasn't sure he'd ever been so close to a trans person before, knowingly. It unbalanced him a little, and he regretted that his own awkwardness, however minor, was adding to hers. He'd get better, and practice made perfect, right? People weren't that different from plants. Millions of varieties, but they all needed water and light. Kindness and a little grace.

"You don't keep any backstock here?" he asked.

"Not much. Mostly the storeroom is stuff, you know—ribbons and pots and extra potting soil and paper towels and receipt paper." She shifted from one foot to another.

"Can you show me?" Hayden asked.

"Umm…sure. Just give me a minute." She ducked behind the counter and through the doorway behind it. Hayden heard a door open and close and a low, urgent rumble of voices. Five or ten minutes passed. Hayden stood behind the register, wondering what he would say if a customer came in.

Melodie reappeared. "Right this way."

After the anticipation, the storeroom was something of a disappointment. Melodie had been right—metal wire shelving screwed to the concrete walls held all sorts of boring requisites to shopwork: bottled water, toilet paper, cardstock for labels, boxes of markers and pens, streamers and ribbons and tissue paper in a full rainbow of colors. Stacks of pots and planters and bags of soil heaped against the wall. Two more doors bracketed the room, one labeled exit, and the other bathroom.

Almost ordinary, except for the two sets of bunkbeds where the shelving ended on either wall. Three of the beds were neatly made up, with denim duvets and fluffy bright green pillows. A rumpled blanket on the fourth gave the impression of a hasty exit, its creased pillow askew.

Hayden scanned the shelves more closely. In addition to bottled water, he spotted granola bars, beef jerky, and fruit and oatmeal cups. At the end of one of the shelves, a microwave and a coffeepot stood beside an assortment of beverage supplies and microwaveable soups and stews.

Without saying anything, he walked to the bathroom door and opened it. The interior was surprisingly spacious, not the utilitarian water closet he'd been expecting. To his right, a plush, if somewhat derelict, armchair stood beside an overflowing magazine stand. Across from that, a shelf was lined with beauty and hair products. A blow dryer hung from a hook. Directly in front of the door was a standard sink, with the toilet he'd been expecting beside it. In the far corner stood a shower with a caddy full of shampoos and body washes. Hooks affixed to the wall held an assortment of colored poufs with matching towels.

Hmm. His first thought was that Rachel was so hard up for funds she was living in the shop, but this didn't look at all like a one-person set-up. He spun slowly on his heel. Melodie hadn't moved from the entrance, her face partially hidden in shadow.

"Who stays here?" he asked.

She shook her head, a minuscule movement. "I think you'd better ask Rachel."

He nodded. He wasn't about to bully her over what obviously wasn't her purview. "I guess that means you don't want to tell me who you were talking to back here, either?"

Melodie shrugged.

He sighed. Weird, but okay. "I'll be back after lunch, then. Thank you for showing me around."

Melodie trailed him to the front door.

Hayden walked over to the same coffee shop where he and Rachel had met. He ordered a grilled sandwich and ate it slowly, barely cognizant of the food in his mouth. Eating was such a chore these days; even the mechanics were difficult. His throat dried out, food stuck to his tongue, and he forgot how long to chew before swallowing. Grieving seemed to steal a person's survival skills.

Something akin to curiosity stirred in his belly. No doubt there was a simple explanation for the furnishings of that storeroom; but for the moment, a mystery beckoned. As far as reasons to live, it was tenuous at best, but he'd take what he could find. Every hour was a victory.

Shelly would want him to make it, wouldn't she? To fall back on the biological imperative if nothing else. One hour at a time, one minute, was the most he could manage right now—and sometimes he failed even at that.

CHAPTER 8

When Hayden jangled back through the shop door, Rachel looked ready for a fight.

"Hello, Hayden," she said in a clipped voice.

He nodded slightly. He was tired, so tired, of the endless, dragging weight of sorrow. Another sensation, something clean and sharp like anger, would be welcome. Plus, he wanted answers.

Melodie was with a customer, not quite managing to look oblivious to his entrance.

"Why don't we step back here?" Rachel said.

He followed her down the short hallway into the empty storeroom. The fourth bunk was now made up as neatly as the other three. Hayden couldn't help noticing Rachel's spine, stiff and taut as an overtightened bowstring. It was hard to associate her constantly roiling energy with hands that could gently untangle angel hair roots and nurture dreaming bulbs through their long sleeps. Rachel Lundgren seemed more suited to life as a lineman than a gardener.

She closed the door and turned to face him. "What do you want to know?"

He laughed but immediately regretted it. The short bark grated in the small space and drained him of the little animus he'd gathered up.

"The obvious, obviously. Who lives here and why?"

Rachel crossed her arms and leaned back against the shelving. "Are you familiar with how the city handles its transgender homeless population?"

That was an unexpected turn. "Uh, no."

"When a transgender woman finds herself homeless, her only option for shelter in this town is with men. And transgender women are at significantly higher risk of sexual or physical assault. The reverse is true for transgender men. They are only allowed to stay in women's shelters. Many would rather stay on the streets than risk assault or deal with the psychological trauma and exhaustion of having their whole identity mocked or erased. Sleeping on the streets is dangerous any time, but when the temperatures drop, it's truly deadly."

"Are you telling me this shop is operating as an unlicensed homeless shelter?"

Rachel snorted. "Of course not. That would be a huge liability. I'm just a business owner with a penchant for hospitality."

"Hospitality? That's a creative way to put it. I suppose Melodie sleeps here?"

"Because she's transgender?" Rachel put her hands on her hips. "Melodie happens to have a terrific, supportive family. She's not homeless."

Hayden didn't blame her for being defensive. This was the craziest thing he'd ever heard. She should be defensive.

"You know this sounds insane, don't you? How are you qualified to do this? What about drug use, sanitation, regulations?" He looked around the room.

"What's dangerous is vulnerable people—kids—on the street with no support systems and nowhere to sleep without fear of being attacked. Most of our guests are teenagers. What should I do, tell them to take their chances outside when I know good and well what's likely to happen?"

Hayden watched as Rachel's hands slid up, her fingers wrapping tightly around her forearms. He took a deep breath, considering.

"How did this start?" he asked.

Rachel let go of her arms and relaxed slightly. "Melodie introduced me to some of the kids at the Unitarian church. There's a community room where transgender teenagers can hang out and connect with local resources. Melodie meets with a support group there sometimes. She's only nineteen, you know. We were talking about the plight of one of the kids after his family kicked him out. Only fifteen and nowhere to go." She shrugged. "We had the space."

We. Hayden's ears pricked up.

"Shelly knew about this?"

"Of course, she did. Shelly suggested it."

Hayden was staggered. His practical Shelly, proposing something so reckless? The woman who dreamed in liabilities and risk analyses? Who refused to even try sushi?

He opened his mouth. Closed it.

"At first," Rachel said, "we operated in rescue mode, focused on a short-term solution for this one child. Quickly, we realized how widespread the problem is, and how scary. If any kid didn't have a safe place to sleep and food to eat, they'd drop out of school almost right away. Fall into God-knows-what to survive— and from there, we might never be able to reach them. But if we can help keep their head above water, at least long enough for them to graduate and make some kind of plan, then maybe they can rewrite their whole story."

Hayden remembered two boys struggling to concentrate on their math homework while their stomachs growled in a single-wide trailer. He knew all too well the desperation of clinging to a plan in the hopes of making it out. Shelly had no illusions about how Hayden and Lorne had clawed their way out of poverty. He would have understood if she had told him about the flower shop, the kids. But she didn't.

"Widespread, huh?"

Rachel shrugged. "We only have room for four beds. It's not a perfect system, and I haven't figured out answers to many problems yet. I try to focus on keeping safe the ones in front of me, the ones under our roof. If everyone else does the same, it can make a difference."

"Are you saying there are more places like this?"

She shrugged again. Clearly, she didn't trust him. Hayden wasn't sure she should. What was the rational, adult response to this? He didn't know.

"What would the authorities say if they knew?" he asked.

"I don't know. Do I look like the authorities to you?" She straightened a box of chips on one of the shelves. "Why should giving someone a bed and a meal be against the law?"

"It's possible you're bringing a dangerous element into the neighborhood and lowering the value of the property. How many of these kids are drug users? Alcoholics? What do you do if there's a fight?"

Rachel scoffed. "The liquor store on the corner or the gas station with its porn collection brings in a more questionable crowd than scared kids looking for a place to sleep. I don't interfere with their business. Whoever is in my storeroom at any particular time of the day or night is none of their concern."

"I can't believe Shelly thought this made any sense. I have a thousand questions about exactly how this works."

"I'm afraid I don't have time to satisfy your curiosity. I have a business to run and customers to assist. Maybe you should do some research on your own before you make a judgment about something you already admitted you know nothing about."

That was a fair point, although Hayden didn't think he needed extensive knowledge to identify countless issues with running an underground safehouse for minors.

Rachel turned towards the door then paused. "You might not understand it, Hayden, but your wife felt strongly about this. You don't have to trust me, but you ought to trust her. Shelly was nobody's fool."

"I'll be back tomorrow," Hayden said abruptly. He needed to disengage, gather his thoughts, and try again later. One thing was certain: he didn't appreciate this stranger trying to school him on his own wife. He was sympathetic to kids trying to scrape by any way they could, but he also wasn't blind to the sort of bad decisions scraping by often entailed. He couldn't just ignore those hazards. As a part owner, he would be liable. But somehow, Shelly had overlooked it.

Rachel's eyes widened with dismay. "Why do you need to come back?"

"This shop is half mine, right? I better get to know how it works. Unless you'd rather I sold my share."

She leaned her head back and took a long breath.

Hayden let her think about it. Any rational person who wanted half-ownership of a florist would shut down her little storeroom operation in an instant, and she knew it. Maybe Shelly had put the section in the will requesting him to keep the share because of the kids. No matter what, he owed it to his wife to figure this out.

He left Rachel standing there, eyes still blazing. "Goodbye, Melodie," he called on his way out the front door. He didn't wait for a response.

Why did he feel like the big bad wolf? He hadn't said anything unfair, had he? Rational. Practical. Common sense. All traits Shelly had exemplified.

Why did Rachel still seem troubled by his presence?

He was missing something. He thought coming to the shop, learning more about what Shelly had been doing here, would make him feel closer to her, but if anything, she was more enigmatic than ever.

It was as if the long tendrils of Shelly's roots, once thick and tangled and burgeoning with fluid and food and strength, had desiccated. They were shrinking, withering, retreating from him across a cracked desert floor, and however fast he ran, he couldn't reach them.

CHAPTER 9

The silence, the emptiness, was inescapable every time he opened his front door. Hayden stood in the frame for a long moment, bracing himself to enter a space defined entirely by Shelly's absence.

He wandered down the hallway to the bedroom. He lay his cheek against the closed door; his palms pressed on the smooth wood. He shut his eyes and slowed his breathing. If he listened closely enough, surely, he could hear her footfalls on the carpet, catch her low voice muttering as she talked to herself like she always did.

What a blessing it had been, how Shelly had filled their closet like trumpet vines filled an arbor. In the early days of their marriage, he was evicted from their bedroom closet; he kept his clothes in the guest room so Shelly could indulge her fashion addictions. For days, he hadn't been forced to face her ghost every time he needed a clean shirt. Now, he couldn't bear to stay away.

He didn't know how long he stood there, caught in a half-dream of impossible possibilities, but at some point, he pushed his way into that room where his wife wasn't.

The room still looked as it had that last morning. The sheets in a clump where Shelly had tossed them off. The closet door open.

He remembered moving around the space as they got ready for work, neither with the faintest premonition that Shelly wouldn't return home.

How he wished there'd been something special, something noteworthy about their tired little rituals that day. If the hospital hadn't given her clothes back to him in a plastic bag, he wouldn't have remembered what she'd been wearing. That bag was in the living room, still unopened. They hadn't talked about anything in particular. He had no last words to cling to. Just *See you tonight*, which turned out to be saddest lie he'd ever heard.

She'd kissed him goodbye, at least.

Hayden walked over to Shelly's side of the bed and sank onto his knees, laying his face on her pillow, where some faint, familiar aroma remained. "Don't go, Shelly," he whispered. "Don't go."

As if she hadn't been gone for days.

He thought again about Rachel Lundgren's bizarre arrangement at the flower shop. What difference did it make what that woman did? She'd been getting away with it this long, however long that was. He didn't care. It had nothing to do with him. Nothing to do with this awful chasm that devoured more of his hours daily, more of himself.

Surely, there were worse ways to imperil a business's viability than helping homeless kids. Hayden didn't think he was paternal by nature: neither he nor Shelly had wanted kids, and while he didn't actively avoid their friends' progeny, he wasn't prone to attract their attention either. But that didn't mean he wasn't sympathetic to their plight. His mother had kept a roof over their heads—barely—but he knew what it was like to feel hungry, to feel cold, to feel outcast. Maybe that was why he kept his distance from kids most of the time. He didn't want to look back at his own childhood, and there was usually precious little he could do to impact anyone else's.

Shelly had found a way to do something. The trans thing was weird, but he didn't know much about it. And at any rate, trans people needed the same things as everybody else—safety, food, water, warmth. Right?

Whatever. He didn't have the energy to think about it anymore. Maybe he'd do some research later. Or maybe he wouldn't. Maybe he'd stay here halfway between the bed and the floor, halfway between life and death, till his bones dried out and crumbled into dust.

That sounded nice.

But the human body was seventy percent water, and that process would take decidedly longer than his knees could hold the position. He readjusted with his back against the bed frame and legs sprawled on the carpet.

A grower. That was what Melodie had said Shelly was. A grower.

From this position, all he could see out the window was the sky. A blue expanse, bereft of clouds, held his gaze. He imagined the trees and shrubs and flowers in the garden, soaking up the last dregs of the season's energy before the frost fell.

Autumn was his favorite time of year. At least, it had been once. He didn't know how he'd endure this one, much less the ones to come.

A lot of gardeners preferred spring, he knew, with its excitement and unfurling. But autumn was about promises. It was about hope. Endurance. Undaunted beauty. Latent strength. Calendars far beyond simple, short human ken.

But what he'd delivered to the earth this year would not return in the spring—not in the form he longed for, anyway. Poetics and biology were cold comfort. He didn't want a philosophical platitude. He wanted Shelly, warm, breathing, and corporeal. He didn't want autumn, didn't believe in spring anymore. He needed his summer girl.

A grower.

Why hadn't he thought of her that way? He was the one with his hands in the dirt and his head in the clouds. The cycles of bees and blooms meant more to him than the Google calendar reminders she sent him for their dinners and dates. He thought she'd been the retaining wall keeping him from wearing away after the deluges of life. But maybe she'd been the soil all along, feeding him and nurturing his meandering roots and straining limbs.

He hadn't considered Shelly's social schedule might be more than courtesy and obligation. Hayden liked people, but he didn't need them much. He tended to slot them into their places and leave them there without much thought. Jason was his assistant, Alex and Eric his foremen. Forepersons, he corrected himself. A Christmas party and a Fourth of July barbecue were his personal obligations to his employees. Shelly's job was more network intensive, so she attended happy hours and dinners, business launches and other celebrations. He'd shown up when she requested his presence. Most of her coworkers were tolerable to share a drink with, and those who weren't, they laughed about on the drive home. Maybe he'd misunderstood what was happening. Maybe Shelly really cared about those people and was trying to stay connected outside the constraints of the office.

He wouldn't have known one way or the other, would he? He tended to check out when Shelly started rambling on about people he didn't know. How much had he missed about the things that mattered to her?

It occurred to him that Blooming Bouquets might not be the only secret she'd kept. Was secret the right word? It sounded so melodramatic. Unacknowledged investment, maybe—although the shop seemed to function more as a non-deductible charitable donation.

They donated monthly to a handful of charities. Shelly did the research, and he'd nod agreeably when she came to him with a list. Refugees, trees, people on death row. He couldn't remember the exact names of the organizations, but he knew they were set up on automatic monthly withdrawal.

Apparently, donating from afar hadn't been enough for Shelly.

Could there be other engagements, other financial relationships he knew nothing about?

He could read her emails and computer history. Look through her phone. Bank statements and credit card bills. He had all her passwords, just as she had all his on a printed list in the safe. He hadn't been tempted to use them before, and he didn't think she had.

Fidelity had been taken for granted between them. Hayden couldn't imagine Shelly betraying him with another man. And as flattering as the attention of other women was, when he noticed it, nobody compared to her. Why would he throw away a lifetime with his best friend for a quick tumble with some bored house-wife hot for the gardener? How sad and trite that would have been.

Hayden rose to his feet and went to the closet, where the safe sat unobtrusively under Shelly's long skirts. He punched in the code, and the door swung open.

Unexpectedly, disappointment swamped him.

The sheet of paper with its neat list of accounts and websites and passwords sat on top of insurance policies and coin folders and passports. Why had he thought there might be something else, a goodbye letter or something unexpected? Shelly wasn't the sentimental sort, someone who'd leave farewells or surprises strewn about. Or so he'd thought.

Hayden looked down at the list with a wry smile. His pass-words were all plant names, no doubt perilously easy for hackers to crack. Shelly's looked like they came from the desk of a CIA operative. He didn't know how she'd remembered any of them.

Even looking at these little keys to all Shelly's locked drawers made him feel vaguely queasy. It felt like a violation of her privacy, somehow. An intrusion. A trespass.

Hayden dragged himself erect and left the bedroom. Maybe tomorrow night he'd sleep in their bed. Maybe not.

He set the list of passwords beside the computer in the corner of the living room and looked at the plastic bag with Shelly's belongings. Her cell phone was in there—probably needed charging. Tomorrow, he would retrieve it. Digging through the clothes she'd been wearing that day was more than he could face right now.

Plans were good. That was something the funeral director had said—keep making plans. Even the smallest task reserved for later would make reaching the next day a plausible reality. And he only had to survive one day at a time.

Hayden walked into the backyard. A dancing breeze fringed with the barest flush of cold tossed the thinning hair on his head and tugged at his shirt. How alive and fresh the outdoors felt compared to his mausoleum home.

He sat down among the snapdragons and sweet alyssum and cried and cried.

CHAPTER 10

"Here." Rachel tossed a green, flowered apron at him. "Melodie's off today, so you might as well make yourself useful if you're going to be taking up space here."

Her words were sharp, but her tone placid. Hayden suspected snark was Rachel Lundgren's native language. Or maybe he brought it out in her. At any rate, she seemed relatively tranquil today, and his own brief bellicosity of yesterday had evaporated as if it had never been.

Hayden didn't know how Rachel managed bookkeeping, but she was an excellent store manager. In addition to the little placards outlining the extent of each plant's care needs, she'd designed a system for employees, too. Beside each plant's name on the price tag were a series of letters denoting which day of the week to water them and a little watering pot icon to indicate how much. This made it simple for anyone to assist customers, regardless of their plant knowledge base. Hayden lost himself in the rhythm, filling his watering can as needed in the industrial sink in the back and moving pot to pot, cleaning off leaves and rearranging displays so the biggest blooms faced the aisle.

Care was comforting. A little water, a little light, a little soil and gravel, and life was inevitable.

Rachel greeted every customer as they came in. Hayden imagined himself working there, now that he had a sense of the shop's inventory and flow; surely, the cash register wasn't too hard to figure out. But he had his own work, didn't he? Besides, summoning a weak smile for browsing strangers was about as much human engagement as he could manage. He was glad Rachel didn't seem inclined to fill up the quiet moments when the store was empty.

Earlier, she handed him a nametag. "What kind of name is Hayden?" she'd asked.

"Could be worse. My brother's name is Lorne."

She swallowed a snort, but not soon enough. "Like lovelorn?"

"It has an *e* on the end, though. My mom read too many romance novels when she was pregnant."

"Those names do have a definite English lord/boarding school ring to them."

"Ironic, since we grew up in trailer parks."

"But Shelly said you went to college. How'd you swing that?"

He shrugged. Funny how long ago that stage of their lives felt —almost as if it had happened to someone else. "I tested well. Got a full-ride scholarship. My brother and I both did."

He didn't elaborate on the hardscrabble childhood they spent taking care of each other while their single mom shuttled from janitor gigs to waitress shifts, but he suspected Rachel's sharp eyes saw more than he meant to reveal.

"Huh. You must have been motivated. And smarter than you look." She grinned crookedly.

"Bored, mostly. I didn't care much about sports or what passed for a party scene, and I was invisible to girls back then."

"But you and Shelly met in college."

"In a 101 Botany class, actually." He remembered how the sun picked stray strands of gold from the thick waves of her brown hair, how her smile flashed like light on water, how effortlessly she drew him out of himself and into her orbit. "She had no reason to be any good at botany," he said, "but Shelly had a knack for succeeding at everything she tried. I thought she glowed. All I wanted was to sit by her for the rest of my life."

He looked away as his eyes burned.

"And so, you did."

"For the rest of her life." Hayden looked back at her. "All this —" he waved his hand. "There's so much I didn't notice."

"She loved you." Some expression Hayden couldn't identify flitted across her features, softened her face.

"I think so. I hope so. But maybe it was more habit than anything else."

Hayden didn't know why he was talking like this, saying aloud things he could hardly whisper to himself. He understood even less why she was listening.

"Love isn't such a bad habit to have," Rachel said as she plucked a dead leaf from a hyacinth plant. "Most people aren't lucky enough to ever be taken for granted."

"I can't say I've heard anyone say that before."

Rachel shrugged. "Perspective of a perpetual outsider, I suppose. Whatever else Shelly had in her life, you were the person she went home to every night. You were the beginning and end of her days. That counts for a lot."

She dusted nonexistent dirt from her hands and moved away from him. "I need to check on something. You okay to watch the front for a bit?"

She vanished into the back before he could assent, and he posted himself behind the counter. From the storeroom, he heard her voice and someone else's rising and falling.

He'd been right, thank goodness the point-of-sale system was fairly transparent, so he was able to muddle through two transactions without calling for help. When she returned, the quietude of her morning mood was gone, and the coiling tension he associated with Rachel Lundgren was back in force and buzzing. Hayden wouldn't be surprised if the tight curls of her black hair had more to do with straight-up electricity than genetic influence.

"Everything all right?"

"No," she snapped. "People are shit."

"Ah, yes."

She wrung out a cloth and began swiping fiercely at the counters, as if the three specks of soil there had personally insulted her. Hayden backed up, leaving her plenty of space for stomping and slinging.

"Mateo's got a black eye and a busted lip. Some assholes said if he wanted to be a man, he better learn to fight like one. Because, obviously, the ability to hurt people and smash things is the definition of masculinity."

Hayden couldn't decide if he should feel defensive or not.

"Who's Mateo?"

Rachel's glinting eyes met his, and he was surprised the air between them didn't catch on fire. "Mateo is the fifteen-year-old I told you about. Sixteen now. His family kicked him out. But of course, it's not enough to be homeless and abandoned by his own flesh-and-blood. Nope, random fuckwits decide his very existence is some kind of threat to their own tiny dicks."

Hayden raised his eyebrows. It was a good thing the store was empty. He didn't think her vocabulary was exactly customer friendly.

"Does he need medical attention?"

"I don't think so. I gave him an antiseptic, an ice pack, and aspirin. What he needs is basic human dignity and respect."

"Yes." Hayden scrambled for more to say. "Are the fuckwits still around?"

Rachel sighed and dropped the cloth back into the bucket of cleaning solution. "No. This happened off-campus when they left for lunch."

Ah, school bullies. Surely, it was at least a good thing they were other students and not predatory adults, right? But Hayden supposed school bullies might be the hardest to escape.

"Should I walk him back to school?" he asked.

Rachel squinted up at him. "You've never met Mateo, and yesterday you didn't want him here at all."

"Nobody should be scared to go to school. If an adult is with him, what are they going to do? Maybe I have my reservations about this whole situation, but that doesn't mean I'd stand by while some kid is being picked on."

Rachel pursed her lips. "I don't know if he's planning on going back to classes. Honestly, I wouldn't."

Hayden spread his hands. "Introduce me. We'll ask. I thought your main goal was keeping these kids in school."

"Ugh. All right."

She led the way, knocking softly before opening the storeroom door. A slight teenager with cropped, black hair sat on one of the bottom bunks eating a cup of ramen. Hayden grimaced when he saw the boy's face. Rachel's description had not done the injuries justice.

"Hey, Mateo," Rachel spoke swiftly. "This is Shelly's husband, Hayden."

The boy looked up, and his face relaxed. His dead wife's name was some kind of talisman, Hayden realized with another pang of bewildered grief.

"I'm really sorry," Mateo said. "Shelly was a great person."

"Thank you."

Rachel stepped closer to the beds. "Hayden offered to walk you back to school if you feel like going."

As Mateo eyed him skeptically, Hayden supposed he didn't look like much from the teenager's perspective. Although he was all lean muscle from a life spent outdoors, he was hardly body-builder material. Add in his wire-rimmed glasses and thinning hair, and he probably looked more like a librarian than a bodyguard.

Mateo shrugged in assent. "I'd like to say I can fight my own battles, but I obviously suck at that. And I have a math test this afternoon."

"All right, then. You finish your lunch, and Hayden will head back with you." Rachel turned and left the two of them alone in the storeroom.

Hayden motioned towards the cup of steaming noodles. "Shelly and I survived on ramen when we were in college. On good days, we'd throw in some cans of bamboo strips or broccoli or something, but most of the time it was ramen and sriracha sauce."

"Ramen and peanut butter," Mateo said. "I'm accidentally becoming a vegetarian."

"There are worse fates."

"Maybe. But I would kill for a chili cheese dog."

Hayden laughed. "I bet I could manage that without any bloodshed. You'll be back here tonight, right?"

"Yeah. Nowhere else to go."

"Well, I'll try to scrounge one up and leave it here. Or with Rachel. Do you know if anyone else is sleeping here right now?"

"We're pretty full up most of the time." Mateo stood, threw away the paper cup, and washed his spoon before replacing it in a container beside the microwave.

"Hmm. I'll see what I can do. You ready to head out?"

"Yeah." Mateo grabbed his backpack and swung it over his shoulder, wincing slightly.

The high school was only a couple blocks over. Hayden's gut tightened as they approached clumps of teenagers along the sidewalks in various stages of social evolution. Navigating school society had been easy for Hayden. A good student and fair athlete, he'd attracted little attention and no bullies while still having plenty of friends. Not that he could remember them well now. Strange to think some people never outlived stages of life he'd all but forgotten. Little lost larvae.

He remembered the cliques, though. Band kids and theatre kids and AV kids. Jocks, hicks, and gangbangers. Nerds and preps and cheerleaders. He didn't remember any transgender kids. There'd been a few gay kids, though. Some who'd apparently decided brassy flamboyance was the best path to survival. At the time, Hayden had thought they loved the attention and reveled in the name-calling, but now he figured they'd probably faked thick skin all along. Others faced the same incessant heckling even when practically curled inside themselves, heads down and eyes shuttered. No way to win.

Hayden didn't think life in his old high school would have been remotely tolerable for anyone transgender. Maybe there had been kids like Mateo and Melodie, and they'd hidden in plain sight from everyone they knew. Surely, things were better now. After all, he hadn't even known what the word meant when he was a teenager, and now there were transgender athletes competing for international awards and transgender actors and widening acceptance of the idea. Wasn't there? It wasn't something he'd wondered much about.

Hayden slid a glance at Mateo's bruised and swollen face. If kids were getting kicked out of their families and beaten up by their classmates, forced to take shelter with strangers because they couldn't find a safe place to sleep, maybe things weren't better at all.

Hayden sighed. He didn't have any answers. He didn't even know why he'd decided to come out here.

Yes, he did. Shelly. Even dead, his wife was still his why.

As they walked toward the school, Hayden glared at every group of kids they passed on principle. He didn't know who the assholes were, but he figured they could all use a little intimidation, such as he had to offer. "You knew Shelly?" he asked Mateo.

"Yeah. She was cool."

"Was she around the shop a lot?"

"Yeah."

If Hayden had hoped Mateo would somehow reveal a secret side to his wife, he was sadly disappointed. If anything, he seemed almost close-lipped on the subject, and the short walk to the school hadn't created a magical bond between them.

Mateo paused on the steps, shifting awkwardly. "Thanks for coming with me."

"Sure. It was nothing. Should I come back when school lets out?"

"Naw. Nobody's going to be here to protect me all the time. I just wanted to make this stupid test. Getting good grades is my only way out of this place."

Hayden understood that. "Okay. Well, good luck with the test, then. I'll see you around."

His arms felt out of place as he walked back to Blooming Bouquets, overlong and swinging the wrong way. What was it about teenage boys that made a grown man foolish and awkward? What would he have done, anyway, if one of those bullies had come after Mateo again? Punched a kid? Lectured them on tolerance?

He smiled. Shelly would have laughed at him. He could picture her incredulous face.

"You've only just left," he muttered, "and I'm already becoming a stranger to myself."

Maybe Shelly was more of a mother than he'd guessed. Maybe there was more than one way to be a father. To be a friend.

CHAPTER 11

Lorne showed up that night with a bag full of supplies Jaciee had packed for him: a twelve pack of Dr. Pepper, popcorn, M&M's, and a box of frozen pizza rolls. Lorne shrugged at the expression on Hayden's face as he piled the items on the kitchen counter.

"I told her Jack Daniels was the more traditional choice, but she said I wouldn't be doing you any favors if I came over and got you drunk. You can feel free to let her know if she's wrong."

Hayden gave a quick grin. "She's probably not. The whole bit about drowning sorrows is something of a lie. If anything, I'm the end who ends up underwater. These days, sobriety isn't such a terrible thing."

Lorne nodded, not looking his brother in the eye as he shook out squares of icy pastry onto a plate and popped it into the microwave. "We can watch a movie, whatever you want."

"Sure." Hayden opened a can of Dr. Pepper and took a long swallow. He barely tasted the sugar on his tongue.

Just as well that Lorne showed up. Hayden might not have bothered to eat at all, left to his own devices. Hunger hardly prodded him, and his senses felt dulled. Colors were dim, and sunrises, more gray than gold.

Lorne was a good brother. Hayden should pretend his efforts mattered; maybe they did.

"Jason said you haven't been coming in much lately."

Hayden nodded, although Lorne still faced the microwave. "I wasn't much use at the office."

"You should have called us. We can take some time off. There's a new pinball arcade downtown. I bet they have a Skee-Ball table where I could whoop your ass like in the old days. You shouldn't be cooped up in here by yourself."

"I wasn't." Hayden sank onto a kitchen chair, cradling his can of soda like it was something stronger.

When the microwave screeched, Lorne retrieved the pizza rolls and set the steaming plate on the table.

"I've been at this place called Rachel's Blooming Bouquets," Hayden said.

"Umm, okay. Is that a vendor of yours?"

"No." He slid a few pizza rolls onto his plate. "It's kind of weird. I found out from our lawyer that Shelly was half-owner in a florist shop. She left her percentage to me in the will and asked me to keep it."

Lorne bit into a pizza roll, immediately howling and panting comically around the piping hot pastry.

Hayden cracked a smile. Every damn time. His little brother had the patience of a magpie.

Eventually, Lorne regained his composure, if not the feeling in his tongue. "Wait. A flower shop? I thought that was your thing."

"Apparently there was a lot I didn't know. Like the woman who owns the other half."

"The co-owner is a stranger?"

"Stranger to me. Not to Shelly. They knew each other for a while, but Shelly never mentioned her to me. Definitely never mentioned the shop."

"Sounds like a mobster setting up his mistress with a little hobby shop of her own." Lorne eyed the plate hopefully but decided to wait a few more minutes.

"What?"

"Oh, you know. On those mobster shows, the guy always buys his mistress some little salon or shop or whatever she wants to keep her happy and available. But they don't usually leave a will asking the wife to maintain the relationship."

"Shelly is the mobster in this scenario?" Hayden tore a pizza roll in half and watched the steam curl up.

"Sure. I mean, none of us really understood her job in the first place. Investment counselor? That could totally be the modern equivalent of import-export businessman." Lorne waggled his eyebrows dramatically.

Hayden laughed. "Shelly would have been thrilled to know you thought she was so mysterious."

Lorne inspected a pizza roll then popped the entire thing into his mouth. "Seriously, what's the deal with the shop? Are you going to keep it?"

"I don't know. I do like the place. The co-owner, Rachel Lundgren, has a unique niche in the florist market, so maybe it will be successful. But we don't exactly get along."

"What's she like? Are you sure you haven't met her somewhere – maybe one of Shelly's work things you always said were so boring?"

"Rachel Lundgren is anything but forgettable. She's knowledgeable enough and driven. Kind of prickly. I'm not sure she has the best judgment. You know Shelly was always the voice of reason wherever she went, and this woman seems to need a lot of that."

"Is there opportunity for recklessness in the world of flower shops?"

Hayden drained the last of his soda and told his brother about the backroom hostel or homeless shelter or whatever it was Rachel was running.

"And when I saw the poor kid with his face smashed in, I was glad they have a safe place to sleep. But using the storeroom of your business to house troubled teenagers is a disaster waiting to happen."

Lorne nodded, his dishwater hair falling over his eyes as it was prone to do. "Most people have no idea how many teenagers are homeless. There's this idea of runaways trolling for drugs or selling sex on street corners, but a lot of kids are couch-surfing and doing their best to get through school despite whatever obstacles are in their way. I see it every day."

Hayden hadn't even considered what his brother's perspective as a high school teacher might be.

"Has this become common in school?" Hayden asked. "It seems like their lives would be much easier if they dropped the trans thing. They're painting a target on their own backs—not to mention dealing with their families. Why not wait till they grow up and get out of the house?"

Lorne snorted. "What if someone said you had to wear women's clothes and go by the name Hollie every day? But you know, only for eighteen years or so."

"That's different. I was born this way. They're trying to reverse the entire process of biology."

"Most of these kids say they were born the way they feel, too —their anatomy just doesn't reflect it. How can a person exist divorced from their own identity? That's not a real life. That's how these kids end up in psych wards, or worse, in graves. Imagine if every day, all the people in your life insisted you weren't real. That you weren't yourself. That's devastating. And dangerous."

Hayden let the words sift through his consciousness. He didn't really understand, but he could let what his brother said sit in the soil a while and see what sprouted. Lorne was a smart guy, and Hayden wasn't inclined to discount anything he said. He wouldn't want to look either Mateo or Melodie in the eyes and tell them they had to hide who they were.

Lorne popped a couple bags of popcorn into the microwave

and filled up two big plastic bowls when the buzzer sounded. "Are you wanting to put the kibosh on this impromptu homeless shelter situation?"

"I don't know." Hayden followed his brother into the living room. "They've got four kids sleeping there almost every night, kids in danger with nowhere else to go. I feel like I can't shut it down unless I have a better solution."

"And do you?"

"I can hardly concentrate on getting dressed right now."

Lorne shrugged. "All right, then. You said yourself Shelly was usually the voice of reason. If she thought this worked, maybe she's right. I mean, obviously it's not ideal, but in the absence of anything else…"

Cary Elwes appeared on the television screen looking suspiciously like Robin Hood.

"*Men In Tights?*"

"Jaciee said to watch something funny. She suggested *Monty Python and the Holy Grail.*"

Hayden shook his head. "You two make the world's worst grief counseling team."

"Sucks to be you, man. We're all you've got."

"Thank God. I don't think I could survive any more help."

CHAPTER 12

He'd forgotten to draw the curtains before he fell asleep the night before. Golden autumn light sifted through the living room window and across his makeshift bed. Hayden could see bronze beech leaves dipping and swaying in the wind. He needed to get up. Needed to go to work.

He'd decided that checking out of his life and responsibilities wasn't an option. It wasn't only about him. Jason, Alex, Eric, and his crews—they needed him to be at least semi-functional. They had families of their own. His misery couldn't be their undoing.

But now, tossing off the blanket felt like an impossible task. His limbs were heavy, even if his eyelids were weightless. He couldn't go back to sleep, and he couldn't rise.

The beech tree did not need to move to thrive; it would stand in the same spot for years. Not only would it survive, but it would sustain countless lives and systems of life. It would breathe and eat and produce and protect and mate. It would communicate with vast networks of roots and mycelium deep underground and commune with the sky and the storms. In constant motion, the beech was likewise immobile. Why couldn't he be like the beech?

Hayden imagined standing barefoot in a bed of loam, his toes taking root and stretching down where Shelly's ashes mingled with life-giving bacteria and dirt, his hands content to rest in the grip of the sky.

Ugh. Without allowing himself another moment to think, he propelled himself up and out of the recliner in a single movement. He staggered down the hall, grabbing clothes without seeing them. He felt hungover when he woke up these days, even though he'd hardly had a drink since the funeral. His eyes were swollen, his head painfully full. He suspected he had cried in his sleep.

Maybe coffee would clear some of the cobwebs. He couldn't bring himself to force down anything to eat. Lunch, he promised himself. He'd eat at lunch. He opened the refrigerator and stared bleakly at the contents. He should take one of the various plastic dishes of comfort food people had made him. Although, by now, they might be bad. He'd hardly cracked a lid since they arrived. He grabbed one at random and stuck it in a cloth lunch sack along with a fork. He'd find out.

He paused on the way out the door, his gaze snagging on the bag of Shelly's belongings still sitting beside the couch. Gritting his teeth, he crouched down and dug out the smaller Ziploc bag jangling with the detritus of Shelly's last day. He left the jewelry and pocketed her phone.

When Hayden opened the office door, an entire cavalcade of expressions passed over Jason's face: relief, pleasure, consternation.

"I thought you were going to take a few days?"

"I took two days and then thought it was time I came back. Are both crews already out?"

"Yup. Days are already getting shorter, but they should have all been on-site by seven this morning."

"We've got a few weeks left to get the plants in. Frost will be here before we know it." The words seemed to echo as they left his mouth. God, why did everything have to spell death, death, death?

"Both teams are on schedule." Jason smiled tentatively.

Hayden could hear what he wasn't saying loud and clear: *You can go back home.* But there was no home without Shelly in it, and he couldn't face Blooming Bouquets today. The Shelly who had walked its aisles was so unfamiliar. Instead of the shop drawing him closer to her, it only heightened the distance between them.

"I'll go through our winter accounts and create a service mailer you can send out for us," Hayden said. "We'll be transitioning soon. We don't want to lose anyone to another company by falling behind."

"Sure."

When he sat down at his desk, he plugged Shelly's phone into the charger beside his computer. His fingers lingered on the battered case, the smudged screen. Shelly's warm cheek had been pressed there. Who was the last person she'd spoken to?

He set the phone down and fired up his computer.

It took an inordinate amount of time, especially considering he was updating and refreshing the same basic brochure he'd used for years; by lunchtime, he'd accomplished the one task he'd promised Jason.

In the break room, he microwaved the container he'd brought. It turned out to be some sort of amalgam of beef and mashed potatoes and various other mushy vegetables. Nothing inappropriately green bloomed on its surface, so he ate it. He barely tasted it. He sprinkled on a thick coating of salt and told himself it was good enough.

Eventually, the mechanics of chewing produced their inevitable result, and he couldn't use the excuse of lunch to avoid Shelly's phone any longer. He closed his office door. Dragged his chair over to the Ficus tree by the window as if that might offer some refuge. Pressed the home button.

Passcode?

Hayden didn't have a passcode enabled himself. He could have sworn he remembered laughing with Shelly about how obnoxious passcodes were. And he didn't use his phone for much besides basic communication and navigation. Their banking accounts were all on the home computer—he didn't use the phone app for that. If someone stole his phone, the most damning thing on there would be his photos, and even those were boring.

But, of course, Shelly's job was much more sensitive than his. Who knew what apps she had downloaded to keep track of the markets, not to mention contact information for her clients? It wasn't as if he even remembered the last time he'd used her phone for anything. It made no sense for him to feel as if she'd slammed a door in his face.

She wasn't even here.

Still, the air reverberated with rejection. His hands shook.

No matter. He had the list of passwords in the safe at home. He'd check that when he got home. No big deal.

He tried to kill a little more time, checking his email, reviewing accounts payable. He could hardly decipher the letters on the screen into comprehensible language. Finally, he gave up, turned out the light, closed the door.

Jason looked up from his computer. "I'll get the winter services brochure out to all our clients this afternoon. Do you want me to work up a new one for prospects?"

"Sure, that would be great, Jason. I'm going to check on the crew sites and then head straight home. Just call me if you need anything."

"Will do, boss."

Hayden felt worse than useless at the crew sites. All he did was interrupt the workflow. He couldn't even take pleasure in the progress they were making. He had to fake his approval— not because he didn't approve, but because he didn't care. And he was afraid his team saw right through his subterfuge.

They deserved better than that. But faking it was all he had to give.

Back at the house, he downed a big glass of water before sitting down at his desk with the list of passwords and Shelly's phone. Without giving himself the chance to stew on it any longer, he tapped in the numbers.

Her background was a photo of the two of them on the Appalachian Trail. When had that been—five, six years ago? They'd backpacked for almost a week and somehow had managed to forget the camp stove. It rained for three straight days. But Hayden couldn't recall when in his life he'd laughed so often or so hard. Why hadn't they taken more trips like that? Why had he let that feeling slip away?

He checked her call log. Most of the names, he didn't know. No surprise. At least sixty percent of her job had revolved around phone calls, and he didn't know most of her coworkers and none of her clients. His own name was far down the list. When he and Shelly needed to communicate during the day, they usually texted. She was always with someone, and his hands were dirty more often than not. Texting was easier.

But Rachel Lundgren's name appeared more than anyone's. That was unsurprising, Hayden told himself. A new business venture, and one in which Shelly had taken a personal interest. No doubt there were all sorts of operational questions to be answered, discussions to be had.

It looked like Shelly had called Rachel every morning on her drive into the office. And then several more times throughout the day, though any sort of regularity ceased after the first call of the morning. This habit, long-established by the look of it, meant Rachel was the last person she'd spoken to on the phone the morning she died.

Of course, Shelly had spoken to other people in person. She'd have said hello to the administrative assistant in the front office, her coworkers as she passed them on the way to her own desk. But then, less than an hour into her day, a stroke had silenced her forever.

Hayden wondered how Rachel had found out what happened on the day Shelly died. The log showed six missed calls from Rachel. What could have been so important that she'd rung again and again? Why did this call log look like Rachel and Shelly needed each other, every single day?

At 2:15 in the afternoon, though, Rachel had stopped calling. Maybe someone else, someone at work, had found out and let her know. But that seemed unlikely. Even if Shelly had discussed her extra-curricular business ventures with a coworker, what were the odds that person would think of calling Rachel during a time of trauma and shock? Or even know enough about her identity to make the call?

No, more likely when Rachel couldn't reach Shelly on her private phone, she'd called the office and been informed of what had happened.

Hayden's mind shied away from the memory of the call he'd received that morning. At first, he had replayed those first horrible hours over and over, as if recounting every moment and detail could unlock a different outcome. Now, he tried not to think about it all.

Maybe he should put the phone down. Maybe this was unhealthy, or dangerous. What is that saying about listening at closed doors? No door was more closed than this one.

Maybe he hadn't been close to her recently, but this was as close as he could get. And God help him, he needed to be close to her.

He checked her text messages next. Like the call log, most of the names were unfamiliar. Jaciee had asked them over for a game night. Shelly's mom had sent an update on a great-aunt Hayden didn't think he'd ever met. Rachel had sent just one text—*Call me when you get this. I'm worried about you.*

If he could've, Hayden would have scrolled back, but if there were earlier messages from Rachel, they'd been deleted. Nausea roiled in his gut.

Hayden read through his own texts to Shelly. Each message left him hollower than the last. So mundane. So pointless. Asking where she'd hidden the leftovers. Reminding her he was going to be home late. Saying *I love you* like he was saying good morning to a stranger on the street.

He backed out of there.

Photos. Shelly liked to take pictures wherever she went, though Hayden didn't know what she did with them. People spent more time taking photos and videos than they did experiencing the actual moment, and what became of them? The pictures stayed locked up in little handheld boxes, sucked into the same empty vortex where people surrendered much of their time and attention.

He needed to take a closer look at her social media pages. The Facebook account where he'd posted that last grim update. Did she have Instagram?

Opening the photos app, he shuddered as if he'd been struck half-senseless by some massive wave of surf.

Images of Shelly and Rachel together, laughing, draped over each other like the best of friends, dominated the thumbnail frames. Here and there were other subjects, but the only story told more often than that of Shelly and Rachel was the story of Rachel herself. The dirt in her knuckles, a constellation of freckles on her cheek, her bare foot wrapped like a wisteria vine around a pale calf he recognized as Shelly's.

Caught in pensive silhouettes, up to her elbows in flowerpots, laughing into the eye of the camera, gazing out across a rooftop sunset on a building Hayden didn't recognize: Rachel was more than subject. She was obsession. Or maybe— Hayden swallowed miserably. She was possession.

There was no escaping the intimacy of the photos. Not that there was anything overtly sexual about them. She certainly had her clothes on in every shot. But there was adoration in the lens capturing her.

Frantically, Hayden scraped his finger down the screen, looking for photos of himself and Shelly. He found a few, perfunctory and posed. In a booth at a bar with friends. Standing outside of a restaurant. Smiling over their twenty-fifth anniversary cake.

There. A photo that looked like a painting. Him in the garden, sunset light falling over his shoulders, his hands deep in turned soil, spent blooms nodding near him.

When she took that photo, she loved me.

He checked the date: almost two years ago.

The loose skin on his abdomen vibrated with agitation so deep-rooted, he thought the foundations of his cells might rattle apart. Carefully, so carefully, he set down the phone, but even so, it shook against the tabletop as he released it. He clenched his hands to still the trembling.

Had she already met Rachel when she took that photo of him? He thought so, but he couldn't be sure. At some point, though, that woman had taken over Shelly's phone, stolen her gaze, held her heart, and kept her secrets. Rachel was the source; she nurtured his wife's hidden life.

CHAPTER 13

Damning as those photos were, the emails were worse. Or at least, Hayden assumed they were. He only read one.

What had begun as a way to hold Shelly close had divided them more irrevocably than even death could have done. It wasn't as if his discovery had opened an abyss. Instead, it illuminated the chasm that had been there all along; now, he was banished to wander the trackless, sunless depths alone.

Hubris, he supposed. That's what he got for imagining he could necromance his wife back to half-life by prowling through her private thoughts. What was a photo, after all, but a penny wish? He had no right to retrieve those from the fountain where she'd dropped them.

He hadn't thought the ache suffusing him day and night could deepen, but it had. He'd pictured their love as a longboat, strong enough for the wildest seas with its oak, tallow, and moss. Now, he saw they were only a paper sailboat with riggings made of string.

If someone asked him what line, what thread of words in the email he'd read from Shelly to Rachel had upset him most, he couldn't have said. It wasn't an overt thing she'd said or any declaration of love. It was how she poured out a complete recounting of her day, her insecurities, and her uncertainties. How she made a confidante of someone he didn't know, as once she'd made a confidante of him. The closeness, inherent and inescapable, in every word. Closeness he'd foolishly considered his and hers alone.

That trail in the Appalachians had been the last time she'd truly unburdened herself to him. Words, thoughts, dreams, and doubts flowed as easily as the countless little streams running under rocks and over roots down the mountainsides. Sometimes, they talked and talked, backpacks bouncing and boots pounding. Other times, they hiked for hours in almost perfect silence, broken only by exclamations over diving kestrels or tumbling waterfalls. Even the silence between them hummed like companionship. Unbreakable, he'd have said, if anyone asked how they were.

But then they came home, and each took a separate path as they had for so long. Hayden found his work so absorbing, so satisfying and consuming, he hadn't noticed the closely woven intimacy they'd shared on the trail was fraying. He supposed if their sex life had suffered, he'd probably have taken notice. Sex had become semi-regular now that he thought about it. That was normal, wasn't it, for long marriages? It wasn't as though they no longer found one another attractive or didn't satisfy each other.

At least, he thought they'd satisfied each other. He was terrified of finding out he'd been wrong. And wrong for how long? He wanted to say he knew they were solid when they took that mountain backpacking trip, but until today, he'd thought they were solid up to the last day. What did he know about solid?

A horrible thought niggled in. Shelly was practical, ordered, and precise. What if the sex he'd thought spontaneous had been orchestrated after all? Intervals spaced to avoid suspicion. Had she been meeting him where they still made sense to each other, or merely keeping him oblivious and content?

Had she wanted someone else, something else, all along? Had she ever been happy? He wished he hadn't charged her phone.

Hadn't opened her computer. Hadn't spent two minutes inside that shop with the woman his wife had photographed with such adoration.

Had Rachel been laughing at him?

No wonder Shelly hadn't told him about Blooming Bouquets. She hadn't been hiding an investment. She'd been hiding a life. Her own, the one she wished she had.

But Rachel had known all about him.

He imagined the two of them dissecting his flaws and idiosyncrasies. His thinning hair and pouchy belly. He thought it was funny and sweet when Shelly bought him nose hair clippers a few months back. They'd laughed about it on and off all night, but maybe she was laughing *at* him—a poor substitute for what she really wanted.

He knew he'd taken her for granted—but wasn't that included in marriage? Keeping a commitment to the one person who will stay committed to you through the many iterations of your humanity? Someone who was simply there, no matter what. Always in your corner, even when they didn't take your side. A friend.

He'd been a friend, hadn't he? At least.

He texted Lorne. He knew his brother would be out of classes soon. And fuck whatever Jaciee thought was the wiser course. He intended to get shit-faced, but not in the house he'd shared with the wife who betrayed him.

He closed Shelly's laptop and shoved it into the hospital bag. The responsible thing to do would be to finish going through it to make sure there weren't any accounts or anything he needed to access. But Hayden wasn't feeling responsible. What difference did any of it make? Everybody died in the end, and love was a lie. A joke played over and over, with the lucky ones ending up in the grave before getting hit with the punchline.

He went to the kitchen, grabbed a box of paper leaf sacks from under the sink. Without giving himself the chance for a second thought, he stormed into the bedroom and flung open the closet doors.

God. How could the closet still smell like her? His brain couldn't accept she was gone, while his body insisted on registering evidence of her presence. He rubbed his nose fiercely and coughed as if he could expel her fragrance.

He pulled her clothes off the racks in armfuls, tossing the hangers aside as he stripped them of their burdens. Skirts and blouses, jackets and blue jeans—he crammed everything into the sacks. He hesitated for an instant when he came to her nightgowns. Confections of silk, lace, and satin a rainbow of colors, a secret between them, he'd thought.

Something in him shifted, and his fingers itched to hold the fabric close and breathe in the scent of her warm body, as if she could be his again and not a stranger. His and no one else's.

Ruthlessly, he squashed the urge. He shoved the delicate fabrics in with the rest of the lot, piled her sneakers and hiking boots and sensible heels on top of them.

He was panting as if he'd run a marathon when he straightened up and looked around at the ruin he'd created. His winter coats hung forlornly in the corner, all he'd left behind when he moved the rest of his wardrobe into the spare room. How willingly he'd abdicated the lion's share of the space for her.

Had he been making room for her, or leaving a growing gap? Well, he guessed he knew which it was now.

Back and forth across the hall he stomped, carrying armfuls of his sweaters and dress shirts and sweatshirts and trousers. Swearing ineffectively under his breath, he spread his clothes out across the walk-in closet, scattering a few items on every rod. He could fill this void all by himself, couldn't he?

It took a few trips, but he hauled the sacks of Shelly's clothes out to the garage and threw them into the bed of the pickup. Desperately, he wanted to hurl them into the bin, but his conscience wouldn't let him. For too long, he'd practiced mindfulness of consumerism and its consequences. The fact that he could even think about philosophy now only made him despise himself more, but the impulse was too strong to counter. Damn if he'd let Shelly's lies push him into increasing the world's garbage quotient. To the secondhand shop her detritus would have to go. They could sort what they didn't want without his input.

Reducing his carbon footprint did not extend to liquor bottles. Nobody was perfect, after all. And gin was made from juniper— that's a connection to the sacred, right? Plus, glass was recyclable. He could grieve like a damn green warrior.

By the time Lorne arrived a few hours later, Hayden was well into the high plateaus of the desert. Gin and tonics sounded excellent, but he didn't have any tonic water.

Lorne grimaced when he came into the house without knocking and found his brother on the couch, swilling gin and clicking through music videos on YouTube. "Dude. It's like the ghost of MTV in here."

Hayden squinted at Lorne. "Get an Uber. You're drinking with me."

"You look like you're already close to the limit. Let's stay in. I could order some pizza."

"Pizza. Yeah. Let's get pizza. I don't want to spend another minute in this house."

"Okay, okay. But don't expect me to get too plastered. I'll have a couple of beers, but I have school tomorrow. And high school students are not kind to hungover teachers. Let me say that again. Not. Kind."

Hayden snorted. "You're so responsible." The word came out closer to *repsonsibibble*.

Lorne tapped on his phone for a minute and sighed as he replaced it in his pocket. He walked into the kitchen and filled a glass with water.

"Here," he said. "Go brush your teeth before our ride gets here. Nobody is going to serve you when you already smell like somebody broke a full bottle over your head. And maybe put on a new shirt."

"Geez," Hayden mumbled. "Okay, Mom."

"Mom wouldn't be nearly as nice as me, and you know it. Now get moving. The Uber is seven minutes away."

The pub they landed at was one Hayden had been in a thousand times before. Sometimes with Shelly alone, but more often with Lorne and Jaciee. Expansive space and comfortable wooden booths gave the craft brewing operation a family-friendly feel. They had a decent menu, a row of old-style arcade games, and six or seven pool tables. Lorne ordered them a pizza, some pretzel bites with hot cheese dip, and a couple of dark ales. And two glasses of water. Hayden scowled, but it was a perfunctory effort. The gin was already sloshing uncomfortably in his gut. Topping it off with a hefty serving of gluten seemed like a wise decision. Something to sop it up.

Lorne was such a good little brother. Hayden smiled fondly at the top of his brother's head as Lorne chased a runaway piece of bread through the bowl of cheese.

"What's up? I'm getting the feeling it's about more than the obvious." Now Lorne was arranging the condiments in a train running down the middle of the scratched and battered table. If Hayden were more coherent, he might have felt a little squirmy about this conversation, but as it stood, he let the words roll right off his tongue without so much as a flinch.

"Shelly was cheating on me. At least, I think she was. I know she was. I'm sure she was."

"No way. Shelly? How'd you find out?"

"Her phone. Her emails."

"Oh." Lorne was silent for a long moment. He kept his eyes fixed on the ketchup bottle as if an explanation were printed on its label. "That sounds—pretty damning."

"Yeah."

"Man, I'm so sorry. That sucks. Who was the guy? Do you know him?"

"It wasn't even a guy. It was that stupid woman at the flower shop. Rachel Lundgren." Hayden tried to put as much contempt as possible into the pronunciation of her name, but it only slurred.

"Oh, shit. Are you sure?"

"Yeah. I mean, no. Not exactly."

"What exactly do you know?"

Hayden told Lorne about the photos, about the intimacy of the one email he'd read.

Lorne still looked skeptical. "Maybe they were best friends. Women are weird with that stuff. The way they hold hands and sit on each other's laps and trade clothes, you'd think they were lovers, but they aren't. I swear, Jaciee's friends wind up half naked or worse almost every time they come over. But it's not a sexual thing. They don't think anything of it."

Hayden clung to that, but only for a moment. "That's Jaciee. Shelly's never been— demonstrative—like that. She has—had— more close male friends than women. And if Rachel were a best friend, don't you think I'd have met her? At least heard her name? She was a secret for a reason."

The pizza arrived along with their drinks. Suddenly starving for the first time since the day Shelly died, Hayden dunked a slice of pepperoni-and-jalapeno pizza in the drippy cheese and scarfed it down. The ale was surprisingly refreshing. He tore a heavily salted pretzel in half and inhaled it with a groan of relief.

Lorne tried again.

"I admit it sounds bad, but you don't know anything for sure yet. There could be some other explanation. I never even saw Shelly flirt with anybody. I can't imagine her cheating on you."

Hayden talked around another bite. "I don't think I would have noticed if she were flirting with another woman. I'd have assumed they were friends."

Lorne turned his still-full glass in his hands. "Did she ever say anything about liking other women? Fantasies?"

Hayden started to say no, but then he hesitated. "I mean, maybe. When we were younger. Nothing crazy, only bedroom talk. I didn't think anything of it. And I'd kind of forgotten. She hadn't said anything like that in a long time."

Lorne heaved a heavy sigh, clearly not happy about what he was about to say. "I totally get if you don't want to keep prowling through her stuff. Do you need me to look?"

Hayden laughed harshly. "I basically destroyed all the evidence. I don't think that's an option. Besides, as gross as I felt looking through her private stuff, I don't want you to."

"Thank God."

For a few minutes, they concentrated on the feast in front of them.

Eventually, Lorne wiped his mouth and plunged back into the fray. "Maybe this isn't something you want the answer to," he said.

"It's not. But is not knowing an option now?"

"It isn't too late to turn back. You don't know for sure Shelly betrayed you. As far as you know, at this moment, Shelly was a devoted wife and your best friend. Nothing you discover now can bring her back. You won't be able to yell at her or hear her side of the story. You won't be able to take it out on her or forgive her. You'll just be left with something that can't be changed or undone. Death took away your future with Shelly. If you chase this, you might lose your past with her, too."

No wonder Lorne was a schoolteacher. Lecturing came so easy to him. But Hayden shook his head stubbornly anyway.

"I can't do that. I can't walk up to the edge of this and pretend I don't know anything. And now I'm in business with Rachel Lundgren. I have to do something."

"You could sell your half of the business and never see her again."

Selling sounded tempting, but he'd want to see Rachel as that news and all its implications sank in.

"Cowardly. That'd make me a coward."

"Deciding for yourself how you're going to remember your

dead wife and how you're going to order your life in the future isn't cowardly. It's taking control."

Hayden shook his head again and immediately regretted it. The room tipped unpleasantly. He took another swallow of ale and pulled the hot cheese closer.

Lorne smiled wryly and pushed the last of the pretzel bites to Hayden's side of the table. "All right. Really, you have only one choice."

"What's that?"

"Talk to Rachel Lundgren. Hash it all out. And not during store hours. You don't know how this will go."

"Ugh."

"Yeah. But that's the way it is."

"No, I mean..." Hayden lurched to his feet. "Where's the bathroom?"

"Oh, lord. Come on."

It was remarkable how much better Hayden felt after puking up his stomach's gin-soaked contents. He splashed cold water on his face and wiped himself off with paper towels as Lorne watched him in the bathroom mirror.

"You're lucky I didn't start sympathetic vomiting. You know I'm not good with this stuff."

"Your sacrifice is appreciated." Hayden thought he might be even more sober. "I think I want more pizza."

"I most assuredly do not. You can have all that's left. But can we agree to switch to water?"

"Sure, sure. Old man."

"Not yet, but I intend to be. Come on. We can play a game of pool before I get you home."

Hayden didn't think he wanted to play pool, but he didn't want to tell Lorne no, either. Once they broke the balls, he managed to almost put the thoughts of Shelly and Rachel out of his mind as he focused on the game. Almost.

Lorne was right. For a little brother, he was right with surprising frequency. Hayden had to talk to Rachel.

CHAPTER 14

Hayden didn't like the rotten feeling that swamped him. As if his muscles and bones were turning to mulch, his brain's impulses were overtaken by a fungal network redirecting its energy to its own purposes. As if he were neither alive nor dead, a beheaded tree stump in a dark forest, its heart soft with stagnant water and decaying fibers, weakly sacrificing the efforts of its dogged roots to mosses and creeping lichens.

Maybe he didn't know the full story of who Shelly was, but he still knew who he was. He was a gardener. A tender of life, not of tombstones.

Predawn birdsong nudged him from his uneasy sleep. He drank a glass of Alka-Seltzer and a cup of coffee and went outside.

He shivered at the frosty chill in the air. The provocation of cold stirred blood in his veins, somehow bracing him against his new reality. He went to his shed and pulled out a variety of implements, leaning them against the door for easy access. He filled the wheelbarrow with mulch and headed to the far corner of the backyard with a metal rake propped on his shoulder.

There was something reassuring in the rhythms of the body

following the course of the sun. Hayden's eyes adjusted effortlessly to the growing light as he worked, cutting down the exhausted summer growth of the perennial flowers, raking away the debris, heaping a deep bed of insulating mulch to grant the sleeping bulbs beneath the earth refuge from the coming incursions of winter. Rays of sunshine soaked through his thin jacket, suffusing his bones with warmth a few degrees at a time. Birds and bugs burbled unbothered around him, as if he were only another ladybug or nodding chrysanthemum.

Here, he belonged. Here, he did not doubt his place. Maybe this had been one of the great appeals of botany and gardening all along. How a person, through all the metamorphoses of their life, barely added to the weight of existence's web but remained inextricably bound up in it. How every creature, every lifeform, was simultaneously irrelevant and fundamental. Each fallen dragonfly took a universe to the earth in its wings, and yet it was still only a dragonfly.

Grief and rage were more than he could carry. But the weight of a wheelbarrow in his arms—that he could manage.

Two hours later, he was dirty and sweating. He rinsed off quickly in a cold shower and dressed for work. No more dropping out of his own life. Maybe two weeks wasn't long enough to learn how to live without his wife, but he'd need to do this for the rest of his life. For one more day, maybe he could breathe through this.

He was going to the office. He was going to the field. He was going to reclaim himself. He was going to talk to Rachel Lundgren and find out the whole truth, or as much of it as he could.

Once he had it, once he'd weighed and turned it over and taken the measure of it, he would bury it. But not like a seed. Not like Shelly's ashes, that even now fed the roots of the little oak tree. No, he'd bury it like radiation in a lead-lined box, never to get out again.

Whatever he'd been mourning wasn't real, so Hayden refused to indulge his grief further. Rage still hovered at the edges of his mind, but he pushed it back as fiercely as he could. Anger was too close to love and sorrow. He needed to keep himself in the in-between. He remembered those first few hours after Shelly had died. Shock and disbelief had insulated him in a weird, surreal cotton wool of numbness. He reached for that sensation now. Numb. He wanted to be numb forever. Warm earth and cold dew and springing roots, these were all he needed to feel.

He wasn't sure where he wanted to meet Rachel. The shop was her home ground. Maybe she'd feel safer talking there, or maybe she'd be more secretive in that place. He could invite her to his house. *His* home ground. Only it wasn't, not really. He had no way of knowing if she'd ever been there before. Maybe she and Shelly had spent long lunch breaks at the house while he was at work; maybe she'd even been in his bed. Only his garden still felt sacrosanct, entirely his own.

He texted Rachel, asking her to meet after the shop closed at the neighborhood park near the high school. Her assent came almost immediately, and she didn't ask why. He wondered if she harbored fear and dread, or if it would be a relief to tell him the truth.

He made it to the office at his usual time. He liked to arrive a few minutes before the rest of the team to start the coffee pot, turn on the lights, and water the plants. Jason would gladly adopt those duties if Hayden asked, but these small tasks helped Hayden feel connected to the heart-blood of his company, however big it grew. And it was important that his employees felt he was alongside them, not over them. Depending on what projects were underway at any given moment, sometimes the crews came by the office first, and other times they went straight to the job sites in the morning. Hayden wanted them to feel this place was theirs. People loved what belonged to them. What they loved, they protected and worked for.

Hayden's mind skittered away from that train of thought.

"Hey, boss!" Jason sounded surprised, and Hayden didn't blame him. He hadn't been reliable recently.

"Hey, yourself. Are those doughnuts in your hand?"

Jason winked. "Two dozen double chocolate. Just felt like one of those days."

"My hangover would kill for one of those."

"Doctor says take two and no need to call him in the morning." Jason set the big paper box down on the breakroom table. "If I feed the heathens once in a while, they're more likely to get me their timesheets on time."

Hayden laughed. "The incentive of getting paid should take care of that."

"You'd think. But you'd be wrong. Occasional chocolate takes the edge off my nagging."

Sure enough, Alex and a few members of both field crews straggled in over the next half-hour, though their actual reason for coming in was somewhat spurious. Hayden suspected Jason had texted everyone that there were doughnuts available if they had time to drop by on the way to their sites. Hayden caught a ride with Alex out to the hospital.

On the way over, Alex kept up a seemingly effortless chatter about the project and the shenanigans of her team. She had a gruff exterior but sharp ears, so little escaped her notice. Hayden was laughing despite himself at the soap opera antics that apparently typified the private lives of practically everyone on the crew. He tended to tune out rather than tune in when people started discussing their weekend plans or the fight they'd had last night. Maybe there was some bizarre comfort to be had in knowing his life wasn't the weirdest one out there.

When he stepped through the doors exiting the hospital hallway into the courtyard, he whistled. "This looks amazing. It's even better than I pictured it."

Most of the crew was already there; several looked up and grinned at his exclamation.

Alex beamed. "It's taking longer than usual, because of the accommodations for the noise levels. But I'm pleased with how much we've managed to get done. We have less than a week left, might even finish a day or two early. The guys have been tireless."

Hayden knew what she meant. Because it was a hospital, they had to consider noise levels, especially during the initial demolition phase of the project. Already, the new garden felt more like peace and shelter, although much of the growth would come next spring.

The many fountains, yet to be turned on, would soon enough need to be shut off to avoid freezing pipes in winter. Hayden wanted this space to be welcoming even in the heart of the cold season, and he adorned the verges and steps of the fountains with potted conifer shrubs. When the anxious or grieving came to the garden for respite, there would always be some green. The small trees, too, were a mix of dwarf flowering deciduous trees and evergreens. Ornamental stones and gazing globes in jeweled hues added color.

Although it was hard to tell while standing in the middle of the garden, Hayden had designed the space so when viewed from above, it had a mosaic appearance, Fibonacci in its pattern. He'd been thinking of bedridden patients, worried family members and friends, exhausted nurses and heartsick doctors, all peering down from the windows, a refuge even for those who weren't physically in it. How little he'd known of grief when he'd drawn these garden plans. Now, as he stood watching the little sanctuary emerge, he sighed with pride.

He rode over with Alex so there would be no checking out early today. From today forward, he meant to do his job and do it well.

Hayden kept his head down, his hands busy, and his mouth shut, and everyone soon relaxed into their ordinary rhythms of work. He had always maintained a strict hierarchy on his sites— the foreperson was the foreperson, whether the boss was there or not. Alex was in charge. If he didn't trust her to follow his plans and direct his employees, he wouldn't have hired her. Once it became clear Hayden wasn't going to shatter into pieces, a comfortable buzz of voices and tools rose and fell in a song familiar to Hayden.

When five o'clock rolled around, Hayden was surprised how quickly the day had flown by. Alex was right; they would finish early. Hayden was proud to see how the crew had risen to this challenge with this project. Sometimes, it was weirdly fun to do something out of the ordinary, even if it was harder. Besides that, Hayden had a longstanding practice of rewarding his crews for any jobs that finished early, whether the contract offered a bonus or not.

Between his early morning exertions and a full day of physical labor, Hayden's back and arms and knees ached. A pleasant weariness, the sort that only comes from hours working in the sun, suffused his limbs. It had been too long since he'd felt this. He tried to hang onto this sensation and ignore the creeping dread winding through his veins at the thought of his upcoming meeting with Rachel Lundgren.

Alex was quiet on the drive back to the office, no doubt tired, too. Hayden appreciated that she was one of those people whose silence was as comfortable as her chatter was easy.

"Thanks for the ride and for putting up with me today," he said as he swung down from the cab of her truck.

"No worries, boss. Always happy for your help. See you tomorrow?"

"I'll probably check out Eric's site tomorrow. But call me if you need anything."

"Sounds good. Have a good night!"

As Hayden watched Alex drive away, he realized he didn't know if she was married, or anything about her home life. He was sure she'd been at Shelly's funeral, but he couldn't remember for the life of him if she'd come alone. Was his personal disconnect from his employees a bad thing? He wasn't sure, but lately, he didn't feel he had an ounce of emotional engagement to spare. It was all he could do these days to stay connected to himself.

When he reached the park, he shoved his hands into the pockets of his dirt-and-concrete-dusted jeans as he strode to the tree-shaded bench where Rachel was already seated, waiting for him. As he'd come to expect, she was a picture of unfurled energy: straight back, tapping toes, clenched hands.

Maybe that's something Shelly had loved: Rachel Lundgren was so *alive*. She was like a time-lapse video of a flower in bloom, always moving faster than time.

Her beautiful amber eyes sparked as she looked up at him. He sat on the opposite end of the bench, crossing one ankle over a knee as if he hadn't a care in the world. Hopefully, she couldn't tell he was trying to hold himself fast to the earth.

"Well?" she said. "What couldn't you have said to me on the phone or at the shop?"

It was as if she wanted him to dislike her, thought Hayden. Well, wish granted. She raised her eyebrows impatiently at him, and any hesitation evaporated.

"Were you ever going to tell me you were sleeping with my wife?"

CHAPTER 15

Rachel's defiance drained away, and her face became completely blank for a moment. Then her eyes filled with tears.

"I loved Shelly."

Hell. Hayden somehow hadn't expected his stomach to drop. He thought he already knew. Thought he was prepared. But he had a hard time speaking over the awful wrenching in his gut.

"That's not what I asked you."

Rachel sucked her lips between her teeth as she chose her words. "We were intimate, yes. I don't know if I would have told you. I thought I wanted you to know, before—." Her hands flapped helplessly. "But after she was gone, it seemed like it would only do harm."

"For how long?"

"Hayden, you're asking the wrong—"

"Don't tell me what to ask."

"Fine. A year and a half."

"When was she going to leave me?"

"She wasn't."

Hayden abandoned the effort to look casual. He swung his foot onto the sidewalk and leaned his elbows on his knees. A few blades of yellowed grass poked through a crack in the sidewalk. A cool wind ruffled his hair.

Rachel hadn't moved. Tears poured down her cheeks, but he had no sympathy for her. He wasn't sure he felt anything at all, besides sick.

His voice came out small and light. "Why?"

"Why what?'

"Why wasn't she going to leave me?"

"Because she loved you."

Hollow laughter pushed its way past his teeth.

Rachel gave one emphatic nod. "She did. She loved me, too, but we spent hours talking about you—who you used to be, who she thought you were. I had made peace with the fact she'd never be all mine. She'd have been miserable if I made her leave you."

Numbness conflagrated in a burst of anger. The thought of Shelly talking about him with this perfect stranger, deciding his future, lying and cheating, all while claiming she still loved him: fury swelled till his head fairly cracked open with it.

"Well, isn't that lovely. I guess I should be grateful. How thoughtful of you both."

"You asked," Rachel snapped. "And I don't have to tell you a thing."

"No, you don't," he said. "In fact, we don't have to see each other again. Do you have the capital to buy out my half?"

"You know I don't."

"Well, I'm going to look for a buyer. There's no reason for me to hang onto it."

"Wait." Rachel shifted and turned to face him. She wiped her cheeks with her palms. "You don't have to do that. You can be a silent partner. I'll send you statements or to your lawyer or accountant. You can forget I ever lived."

"Why should I help my wife's lover run the business my wife bought her? You must know how crazy that is. I don't ever want to think about you again, much less account for you on my taxes."

Her face worked as she fought for composure. "It's not about me. This was important to Shelly. She wanted us—you and me—to have this piece of her together."

Hayden stood. "Oh, now you've really miscalculated. Do you think I care about what Shelly wanted? She lied to me. She hurt me. And now, after finding out I was sharing her against my will, you seriously think I'm gonna hang onto some kind of shared memory for her?"

He strode away, shaking out his hands as if he could shake out everything he had learned. He slammed the driver's side door of the pickup and rested his head on the steering wheel, trying to gather his thoughts. Trying not to rattle apart into a thousand pieces.

Had he known his wife at all? He'd been so sure there were no secrets between them, at least none bigger than candy stashes. It wasn't the lie itself that was so stunning, not even the idea that she'd been having sex with a stranger. A woman. It was the months and months and months of maintaining the lie. Of lying beside him and looking him in the eye and getting dressed and undressed together as if nothing stood between them.

Had she not felt guilty at all? What had he done that she felt justified? They hardly ever fought, and not over anything important. How could that woman claim Shelly had loved him when every single day, she'd wounded him without an ounce of remorse? It was as if he'd been dying of a thousand cuts and hadn't even realized he was bleeding out.

But Shelly knew. And she'd gazed down at those welling cuts with no intention of stitching them up or slowing the flow.

All those years he'd counted fidelity as part of his due. When other women hit on him, which wasn't often, he told Shelly, and they laughed about it together as if there was no universe in which he'd ever cheat on her. And there hadn't been, as it turned out. But why? What had been the point?

Not that he'd missed out on anything, exactly. There wasn't some what-if bombshell rattling around in his memory, nobody he secretly pined for. He could have had meaningless sex every week with a new stranger, and it wouldn't have taken the agony out of this injury. He'd still thought fidelity was part and parcel of the deal they made to be partners and grow old together and keep each other safe.

You couldn't be partners with someone who was busily digging the ground out from under your feet when you weren't looking. Couldn't be safe with someone who handed your soul and secrets over to someone you didn't know, who lay naked in bed with another woman and dared to say your damned name as if it still tasted like love in her mouth. And he sure as fuck didn't have to worry about growing old with Shelly now.

No matter how Rachel protested, Hayden didn't believe for a minute Shelly wouldn't have left him eventually. Rachel probably thought he was less likely to sell the shop if he believed Shelly had intended to stay with him. Rachel had no reason to protect him, only herself.

He'd been their fool long enough. He was done with that.

No point in making good decisions now. He drove through a fast-food drive-in and ordered a sack full of every greasy, crunchy thing on the menu that struck his fancy, along with a bucket of full-sugar soda. He turned the radio up and ate whatever he could grab from the sack as he rambled up and down the city streets, licking the salt off his fingers and singing along to classic rock.

He didn't want to go home, and after a while, he realized he was zigzagging between various worksites he'd designed and managed over the years. As if sizing up the girths of tree trunks and evaluating the maintenance of flower beds he'd planted could lend meaning to lost vows and broken promises. As if dirty hands and a tired back and things that grew in the sun could make a life out of wasted years.

He wanted to see something he'd poured himself into that lasted and breathed. Still flourished, multiplied, and thrived.

When his phone rang, he wiped his fingers on his jeans and answered. "Hayden Hill here."

"Hayden, can you please come to the shop? We need help."

The words were garbled between sobs, the voice barely familiar.

"Who is this?"

"It's Melodie. Please, please come."

Whatever was happening, it had nothing to do with him. Still, adrenaline surged at the panic and fear in Melodie's voice. Hayden fought the urge to rush over. He knew even less about this person than he knew about Rachel. Although, he liked her much, much better.

"Call Rachel. It's her shop."

"I tried. Her phone is turned off. Please, Hayden. I don't know what to do."

Hayden turning the truck around in a strip mall parking lot and headed back toward Blooming Bouquets. "What's going on? Do you need to call 911? Is someone hurt?"

"I can't call the police. Just please come. Please."

"I'm on my way."

"Come to the back door. The shop's closed up for the night."

The skies had dimmed, and his automatic headlights switched on. What could be going on at the shop?

He'd known the storeroom shelter was a terrible idea as soon as he'd seen it. It was only a matter of time before all Rachel—and supposedly, Shelly's—good intentions went south. A fight? A theft? Vandalism? Hopefully not a medical emergency. Surely, Melodie would set aside her unreasonable fears of the police and call if someone needed immediate medical attention.

He didn't really know why Melodie didn't want to call the cops—possibly to avoid getting Rachel in trouble. But kids, especially vulnerable, at-risk kids, shouldn't be in the position of keeping secrets for adults. Though, Melodie was a young adult, at least nineteen or twenty.

Still a kid to Hayden.

He muttered to himself as he drove, furious that right after breaking ties with Rachel for good, he'd been sucked back into her drama. Melodie had sounded terrified, and he didn't have the heart to ignore her. He'd worked himself up into a self-righteous dudgeon by the time his tires squealed into the parking lot.

He sprinted around the corner of the building and banged on the back door, belatedly hoping he didn't need some kind of weapon. He didn't carry a gun, but he could have grabbed a pair of hedge clippers.

Melodie practically fell out the door before pulling him in. She must have been waiting for his knock.

"Thank you for coming."

Hayden blinked as he looked around the small space and got his bearings. It was made smaller by the presence of two people he didn't know, as well as a badly bloodied Mateo. The slight teenager was seated on one of the bottom bunks, hunched over and holding a cloth over his left eye. Blood swelled from his mouth and nose and dripped onto his shirt.

"Shit." He crouched on the toes of his work boots in front of the injured boy.

"Same kids?" he asked. Rage thundered in his chest as he looked at Mateo, small and broken, but he kept his voice gentle.

"Some of them." Mateo's words were hard to understand through his swollen lips.

"May I?" Hayden gestured to the cloth.

Mateo dropped his shaking hand.

He couldn't help grimacing at what he saw. It looked like someone had stomped the boy's face in. One eyelid was swollen shut, and bruising spread down his cheek.

"We have to get you to a doctor," he said.

Mateo shook his head.

"His parents kicked him out," Melodie said. "He doesn't have money for a doctor. And the police—"

"Doctors can't refuse emergency care," Hayden said. "Mateo, you can put me down for the billing. And the police can help you. I'm guessing this didn't happen here?"

"No," Melodie said.

"Then you don't have to tell them where you're staying,

Mateo. Just tell them what happened. You need to bring charges against these guys, or it's going to get worse. Or don't. The police won't be able to do much but ask questions if you don't feel like telling them anything."

Hayden addressed the others in the room. "We can discuss what to do about the police later, but right now, I need to get him to a doctor. You called me to help. This is what help looks like. I have room in my pickup for two of you, so who's coming?"

"I'll come," said Melodie.

Hayden looked over the other two teenagers. Were they old enough to be in high school? Makeup only made them look younger, like little kids at their mom's dressing table. Were they both girls? He wasn't sure. Honestly, they would have fit in with any number of cliques he remembered from his high school days —the goths, the glam rockers, the theatre kids. Fleetingly, he wondered how many of those easily accepted identities had served as covers for trans kids.

God, life was hard. So much harder for some than others.

He nodded in their direction. "I'm Hayden."

"I told them who you were," Melodie said.

Hayden wondered what that meant. Who he was. Rachel's partner? Shelly's husband? The cuckhold? Or just a helper?

"Sage."

"Valkyrie."

Sage had on the most makeup, but her—their?—gender was least distinguishable to Hayden's eye. Valkyrie hugged herself, bouncing anxiously up and down on the balls of her glitter-sneak-ered feet.

"Will you two be okay here by yourselves? Do you feel safe?"

Sage laughed shortly. "Safety is a spectrum. Safer than out there. We'll be okay."

They slung an arm around Valkyrie, whose movement slowed. Sage was a natural nurturer, Hayden recognized. How could compassion come so easily to some people while brutality came so easily to others?

"Don't worry about us. Help Mateo. We'll be here when you get back."

Hayden looked questioningly at Melodie, who was already sliding into her jacket. "Lock the door behind us," she ordered as she slipped an arm under Mateo's shoulder and helped him to his feet.

All right, then. Hayden didn't have much choice but to trust that this ragtag little family knew what they were doing. Hopefully, they were right about him, too.

He turned on the radio in the pickup, hoping a few tunes might distract Mateo from at least a small measure of the pain. They were only a few minutes from an urgent care center with late night hours. Emergency rooms had long waits, and significantly more exposure, which Hayden instinctively wanted to avoid for Mateo. The paranoia these kids carried must be infectious, he thought.

Melodie sat ramrod straight against the passenger window. Occasionally, a dark profanity would burst from her lips, but mostly, she tried to restrain her anger in lieu of consoling her friend. She held Mateo's right hand tightly in both of hers.

Hayden kept his eyes on the road, his stomach churning. What would possess one human to do this to another—and for no other reason than being different.

Hayden had never been unaware of the fortune and misfortune of his birth. Poverty and neglect were weights he carried as a child, but neither his gender nor the color of his skin counted against him. Watching his mother attempting to scale walls he would always be able to circumvent had left a clear impression. He remembered well the humiliation a boy suffered listening to the talk of men, seeing their gazes slide over his mother like grease, shuddering when she didn't flinch at the touches she couldn't avoid.

He didn't want to be like those men. As a child, he'd often blamed his mother, but as a man, he understood the impossible paradoxes of her survival and the survival of her two boys. He didn't ever intend to be the cause of those paradoxes for any other woman. He had a zero tolerance for sexual harassment on his job sites, or among his friends. Lorne, he knew, was the same. Some hard lessons couldn't and shouldn't be unlearned.

From what he remembered, nobody wanted to be called gay in high school, and dyke was a common epithet for any girl who dared to reject a boy's overtures, but there had been a handful of kids Hayden was sure were homosexual. They'd mostly kept to themselves, surviving the bullying and ostracizing with a ragged, holey cobweb of other outcasts. Hayden had hardly given them a second thought.

Transgender hadn't even been a thing—or at least it hadn't been acknowledged as a thing by anyone he knew. Drag queens made occasional splashy appearances in music videos and French Quarter parades, but that was about the extent to which he'd ever personally been confronted with the issue. It had never occurred to Hayden to wonder what it would be like to find himself trapped in the wrong body, in a form that horrified and repulsed and frightened him. To dread showers and locker rooms and the sensation of his own skin under the sheets. To be so alone, even the person in the mirror was a stranger.

He'd like to think if he had known someone like Melodie or Mateo, he'd have at least been kind even if he was confused, but he doubted it. He wasn't a bully in school, but he might have laughed at the idea of someone being the wrong gender. He was no different from anyone else in that respect, having no understanding at the time. And how could anyone understand what they weren't allowed to admit existed, much less actually talk about?

He glanced at Mateo. The boy's eyes were closed, his fists clenched. Hayden thought he was trying to control his breathing. Hayden hoped the kid wouldn't suffer a panic attack on top of everything else.

Thank God. Only a handful of cars were parked outside the urgent care, and according to the sign, they were still open for another hour. Hayden pulled the truck in and parked as gently as he could, not wanting to jar Mateo.

"All right, buddy, we're here. We'll have you feeling better in no time."

Even to Hayden's ears, the words sounded like a lie. But what else could he say?

CHAPTER 16

Hayden and Mateo were stuck at the urgent care long after the front doors were locked. Even so, after a harried doctor finally looked at Mateo's injuries, he sternly ordered them over to the ER, where they sat and waited some more, shuttling between exam rooms and imaging rooms. Once the news came back that Mateo's orbital bones were fractured but not broken through and no surgery would be necessary, Melodie called her parents to come pick her up. Hayden wondered if he should offer to walk out to the parking lot to meet them, but he didn't want to leave Mateo alone.

It turned out there wasn't much the doctors could do for an orbital bone fracture. Ice and painkillers were about it. They stitched up a couple of cuts and prescribed antibiotics that Hayden could pick up at the twenty-four-hour pharmacy on the corner.

Hayden didn't like the way the nurses and doctors eyed him, but he couldn't blame them. An older white guy taking financial responsibility for the bills of a vulnerable young brown kid with no permanent address? Hayden hadn't even considered the sex-trafficking side of the story when it came to trans kids out on the streets, but he considered it now.

That was probably a whole fetish of its own. God, he hated people tonight. Anything he tried to say to these strangers protesting he wasn't that guy would only backfire, though—the whole protesting-too-much thing. He gritted his teeth, held Mateo's hand, and ignored their glares and sniffs and curt replies to his questions. He left the room with alacrity when the doctor arrived, partly to give the kid privacy and partly to allow the doctor to run through all the abuse questions he needed to ask.

That feeling didn't ease up any when the cops showed up. Hayden didn't know if he was irritated that the staff thought he was a potential threat or grateful they took their mandatory reporting duties seriously. He was just a Good Samaritan, he told the officers, driving by in time to see some unidentifiable toughs running away from a prone Mateo. And Mateo wouldn't say anything at all.

Hayden didn't know what, if anything, they believed. They seemed equally repulsed by Mateo as by anyone who'd help him and insisted on referring to Mateo as "she" through the whole ordeal. Hayden gave them his card and told them to call anytime if they had more questions, but he doubted they'd devote much more time to the plight of a kid they clearly despised.

Mateo, Melodie, Sage, and Valkyrie must live in an eternal state of exhaustion, he thought, from nothing more than bearing up under the cold looks and terse tones of so many people they encounter every day.

It was almost midnight by the time they left the urgent care center and got the prescription filled. Mateo's mouth was too sore to eat real food, so Hayden took him through a fast-food drive-thru and nabbed a couple of chocolate milkshakes and some fries. Fries didn't require actual chewing—they were basically melt-in-your-mouth sticks of salted grease. Even sucking on the straw made the boy flinch, but chocolate appeared to be worth the pain.

"I'm worried about you. What do you think about coming back to my place and spending the night there? Just to make sure you don't have some kind of bad reaction or need something in the night."

Hayden hoped he didn't sound creepy. After the way the people in the clinic reacted to him, he felt creepy. But he was seriously worried about Mateo. He had to offer.

The boy shook his head, then winced at the motion. "Naw. Sage and Valkyrie will worry."

"What about your parents? I know things aren't great there, but wouldn't they want to know you're hurt?"

"No way, man. My dad views me as a personal affront to his own masculinity, and my mom thinks I'm going to hell. They're the last people I'd ask."

"We could text Sage and Valkyrie to let them know you're okay. You could get a real shower, sleep in a bed instead of a bunk. I can drive you to school in the morning."

"Look, I appreciate your help, but I want to go home now." Mateo took another slow, painful sip of his milkshake, leaned back, and closed his eyes. Hayden's gaze caught on the boy's torn and bloodied tee shirt, how the red ooze soaking into the khaki fabric had faded to a muddy brown.

Hayden put the truck into drive. It made his heart hurt, how this kid called a storeroom in the back of a strip mall home, how the people who should have been his shelter were his greatest threat. Hayden took an extra five to pull into a 24-hour gas station where he could run in and buy a clean shirt intended for drive-by tourists. Mateo's weak smile when Hayden pressed it into his free hand only deepened that ache in his heart.

The shop was only a few minutes away, but by the time Hayden parked the truck, Mateo was fast asleep—no doubt the combined effects of an adrenaline dump and whatever pain medication the doctors had given him. Hayden left the truck running for a few minutes, reluctant to rouse the exhausted teen. Streetlight filtered through the windshield over Mateo's delicate features. In sleep, he looked even younger than his fifteen—

sixteen?—years. Hayden couldn't remember the birthdate Mateo had rattled off to the triage nurse.

Hayden and Shelly hadn't wanted children of their own, and that wasn't a decision he had ever regretted. Jaciee and Lorne were trying, and his brother desperately wanted to be a father. Maybe Lorne thought he could undo everything their father had done to them, or maybe he just loved kids. He was a teacher, after all. Hayden knew the paternal urge gene had skipped him entirely. Nothing about the current state of the world, ecologically or politically, screamed *let's make more of us,* as far as Hayden was concerned.

Still, as he watched Mateo sleeping in the passenger seat, something stirred in him, something protective and perturbed. How were this child's parents willing to let him starve, freeze, or simply disappear because he wouldn't fit into the shape they intended? They didn't understand why Mateo was the way he was—did they have to? Human beings understood perilously little of the world in which they lived. Rejecting everything confusing would immobilize humanity with ignorance.

Hayden supposed humanity was mostly incapable of growth yet still unwilling to wither away. Like a larger plant robbing seedlings of sunlight, sucking down nutrients, stubbornly keeping their buds furled.

All his life, Hayden had heard people justify their treatment of people on the street by insisting the homeless had already given up on themselves. They won't help themselves, they won't take their meds, they won't get a job, they won't try. Hayden didn't how people could be so sure they understood someone else's reality.

Hayden didn't think Mateo and Sage and Valkyrie had given up on themselves. It looked to him like the opposite were true: they were fighting for themselves, fighting for their identity, something most people never had to contemplate. They had to fight to get their meds and to be allowed to take them. They were kicked off teams and turned away from job interviews. And at night, they had no safe place to sleep. No family to tell them tomorrow morning would be brighter, to hold on and things would get better. No one to love them no matter what.

Hayden felt ashamed for thinking Melodie was lucky her parents supported her and kept her from a similar fate, when that should be the bare minimum any child could expect from parents. He knew firsthand, though, how flawed parents were. Procreating didn't automatically make a person compassionate.

Well, he couldn't solve this tonight and thinking about how he could possibly help was pointless at this hour. Not that he had any reason to think he had something to offer. One straight, white guy who couldn't keep from crying for more than a few hours was probably worthless to the discussion.

"Hey," he said in a quiet voice. He didn't want to shake Mateo. Who knew how traumatized the kid was? "Mateo. Time to wake up."

Mateo blinked and straightened up.

"Do you want the rest of the milkshake?"

"Naw. My stomach doesn't feel so good."

"Should I go in with you?"

Mateo shook his head. "They're probably asleep. I don't want to wake them up."

"Okay. I'll see you around. Are you going to school tomorrow?"

Mateo shrugged. Hayden figured the boy should probably sleep instead, but that might be difficult with the shop open. He resisted the urge to offer his house again. When had he developed this weird tendency toward hospitality, anyway? The last thing he wanted was to put up with another person in the house haunted by his dead wife.

He watched Mateo limp across the alley to the back door, his new tee shirt tucked under an arm. The boy pulled a key out of his jeans and disappeared inside. Without a doubt, he'd remember to lock the door behind him.

As Hayden navigated the dark streets home, his hands shook, and tears filled his eyes. He didn't know who he was crying for, a brutalized child alone in the world, a dead woman who'd left a trail of lies behind her, or the man who stood outside of them both.

CHAPTER 17

By ten the next morning, Hayden was strongly tempted to block Rachel Lundgren's number. He wasn't avoiding the woman; they needed to talk about Mateo and all the kids who took refuge at the flower shop.

But not right now. Right now, he was working. If he was going to retake his life, compartmentalization was key. Maybe other people could juggle multiple existential crises and emergencies and planting flowers and paying bills, but he couldn't. One thing at a time.

After talking to Rachel, he was afraid he'd never sleep again. Insomnia had dogged him since Shelly died; now, he replayed every touch and conversation against a backdrop of infidelity and lies. He fully expected to stare grit-eyed at the ceiling for the rest of his life. But last night, he collapsed as soon as he got home. He hadn't even made it out of his dirty jeans.

As he drove to the office, he found himself adrift in a sea of time. Pulled in and pushed out by tides whose calendars he could not measure. His conversation with Rachel might have been ten years ago or ten minutes ago.

His hands on the steering wheel looked strong and powerful—

the hands of a man who wrestled with the earth. But he felt bowed and ancient. He might be a pleated inkcap mushroom, fated to live and bloom and burst into death in only a few hours, or a yew tree standing for hundreds of years, its heart hollowed out and rugged trunk robbed of the mercy of battering storms and sudden ends.

He'd go on as he'd begun and show up in body if not in spirit for his employees. How he felt had nothing to do with needed to be accomplished each day. So, again and again and again, Hayden steered his mind away from the deadfalls and quicksand of broken hearts and buried ashes and focused on the tasks at hand. He even managed to pull off a meeting with a new client. Unlike his regular customers, they knew nothing about his recent loss and had no compulsion to offer condolences. What a relief that was.

Some days he hated everyone who didn't acknowledge the giant hole in his chest, and other days he hated everyone who couldn't help staring and poking at it, as if their meager Band-Aids could stitch it up. Today, it was a weird sort of balm to be in a room with someone who wanted nothing from him but the labor of his hands, who didn't care one way or another what kind of day he was having or what hurt he was carrying.

At lunchtime, he finally relented and sent Rachel a text message saying he would come by the shop after work to talk. She didn't respond, but at least his phone stopped buzzing.

By the time he found himself back in the driver's seat of his truck, the impetus propelling him that morning had evaporated. The ruthlessness he used to push away thoughts of Shelly crumbled without warning into despair. A great vapidity swallowed his limbs. Why had he felt invested in Mateo, Melodie, and the rest of the kids he'd just met?

He didn't think he cared about anyone, least of all himself.

Hayden wasn't sure he had enough energy to expand his ribcage for one more breath, much less the inclination to jump into someone else's fight. What could he do, anyway? He didn't know the first thing about what they were facing. What was the point?

Still, he'd told Rachel he'd come by. And forcing himself to drive the few blocks over to see her seemed easier than cancelling and dealing with the fallout.

He'd show up, answer her questions, and then drag himself home and sit through the hours waiting for him there.

He wasn't prepared for the reception he got when he came in. Melodie stood watering the plants by the picture window, and she greeted him with a glittering smile.

"Hug?" she offered.

He opened his arms with a shrug. He'd never been much of a hugger, but the past few weeks he'd learned to endure them. Virtually everyone was hugging him at the funeral. Jaciee. Even Lorne. Melodie's arms were strong, and she held on longer than he expected. And he found himself relaxing and hugging her back.

Damn it. His eyes were wet when he pulled back, but she pretended not to notice. She returned her attention to the flowers as Rachel came forward. Hayden expected her to be full porcupine, but her usual humming energy was dampened, her gaze sober rather than angry or defensive.

"Do you mind if we talk in the back?" she asked.

He nodded and followed her into the storeroom. Her two braids, fat and gleaming, bounced over her shoulder blades. The room was empty, and the bunk beds were neatly made up. Hayden wondered whether Sage and Valkyrie attended school or were out on the streets or working. He'd barely gotten a look at them the night before and had no real sense of their age beyond not nearly old enough to be alone.

Rachel turned to face him; her honey eyes were uncharacteristically soft.

"First, thank you for helping last night. I never turn my phone off, but after—" she swallowed. "After yesterday's conversation, I wanted to disconnect. Naturally, I picked the worst possible time. I don't know what would've happened if you hadn't shown up. Kids don't always make the best decisions on their own, even smart kids. Thank you."

Hayden waved his hands vaguely, disarmed by her gratitude. "What else could I do?"

A little spark of the Rachel he knew flared. "You could have said it wasn't your problem and ghosted. You could have called the cops and made it their problem. But you didn't. Just say you're welcome."

He smiled. "You're welcome. How was Mateo this morning?"

"Really hurting. I gave him some ibuprofen and acetaminophen, but I don't think he'll be feeling better any time soon."

"Did he go to school?"

Rachel shrugged. "I don't know. Rules are they must be out of here by eight o'clock since the shop opens at nine. I hope so, but I wouldn't blame him if he posted up on a park bench and went back to sleep."

"Rules, huh?"

"Have to keep some kind of framework in place. And it's good for them to have structure to work around. There are occasional exceptions, of course."

"Did you talk to him about letting the police help?"

Rachel's lips tightened. "I asked. He said no."

"That's a mistake. If they get away with an attack like that, they'll be emboldened and come back for more. Or go after someone else."

"Well, that didn't take long."

"What?"

"Somehow it always becomes the responsibility of the victim to undo all the wrongs in society. If the rape victim doesn't report and testify, then it's their fault when the rapist reoffends. If Mateo doesn't report these guys, then it's his fault when they continue to be assholes."

"That's not what I meant at all. I'm trying to help here. I don't want to see this happen to him again—or worse."

"I get that, but you can't be one more person taking Mateo's agency away from him. He needs to decide how he's going to deal with this."

Hayden sighed. "What's your solution, then?"

Rachel glared. "Believe it or not, I don't have a handy little solution to violent hateful people in a systemically discriminatory society right here in my back pocket."

"There has to be something we can do."

"There's lots of things we can do. We can help and support Mateo. We can provide safe spaces for all people. We can write to our legislators. Attend local city council meetings and town halls to argue for homeless and domestic abuse shelters that aren't based on an examination of people's genitalia. Show up and speak out. But we can't bully victims into doing what we want."

Hayden shook his head. "I wasn't going to bully Mateo into anything. Did he say I bullied him last night?"

"No." Her voice softened. "He said you were great last night. But make sure you don't undo the good with some savior-I'm-gonna-fix-it-all complex."

Ouch.

Rachel tilted her head. "There is something you could do. On Thursday night, there's a town council meeting. One of the items up for public comment is a new ordinance that would require people seeking shelter to submit to a strip search. You could show up and speak up there."

"Maybe I will. Will you be there?"

"Of course. Melodie and her parents are coming. I think some other people from the support group will be there. The bigots will be out in force, so the more people we have willing to speak on our side, the better. This is one case where having a straight, middle-class white guy who can speak in complete sentences would be a good thing. The council needs to know that a safer society for trans people is a safer society for everyone."

Panic bubbled at Hayden's fingertips, like dew evaporating from rose petals in the sweltering summer sun. He barely knew what the issues were, much less where he stood or why. Speaking in complete sentences suddenly seemed like a tall order. He didn't think anyone should face violence or risk freezing to death simply because of who they were, but that was about the extent of his philosophy on the subject. Driving Mateo to a police station to fill out some paperwork was a far more comfortable notion than standing up in a room full of strangers and maybe even news cameras to throw his support behind people whose choices he didn't understand himself.

"Maybe," he said again.

"If you decide to go," said, "you can meet me here to ride over together. Six o'clock. The hearing starts at seven, and we should get there early."

"Sure." Hayden scrubbed his hand over his eyes. Fatigue was like a boulder on his shoulders. He didn't understand why exhaustion was so constant and overwhelming these days. He'd be dead on his feet all day and still unable to sleep at night.

Unexpectedly, Rachel rested her hands rested on his forearm, like a dragonfly alighting on a reed of sweet grass. "Anyway, thank you for showing up last night and doing the right thing. You won't need to do that again. I'll keep my phone on. But I appreciate what you did. I know it wasn't easy for you, after everything."

"Anybody would have done the same—except for those bozos who beat Mateo up, I guess."

"You'd be surprised." Rachel crossed her arms over her chest. "The high and mighty find many ways to reason how the love of God necessitates the hatred of people. Or turning away from them." She chuckled slightly. "You'd better get out of here. You look like you're about to fall asleep on your feet."

As he drove away, Hayden realized he liked it better when Rachel was all prickles and poison and didn't know how to take any kindness from her. He rolled down the window and turned up the radio to stay alert. Luckily, he didn't have far to drive—another benefit of life in a small town. No soul-sucking commutes, hours spent on the road. No, he and Shelly had wanted an accessible life.

They'd deliberately chosen a home where they could walk or ride a bike to most places they might want to go—the corner pub, local grocery, farmer's market, or library. What passed for the downtown district was only fifteen minutes away. Hayden did the most driving for work, with various sites in nearby towns.

Sadness swelled in his throat, threatening to choke him. They'd been so thoughtful about building their life together. They had seemed to hold their happiness with both hands. Other people they knew got tangled up in debt ladders and consumer religions, but not he and Shelly. They did work they loved and spent their money on intangibles more often than on stuff. They tried to live sustainably and leave their trails greener than they found them. How much of their happiness had been an illusion only he had believed?

Something was missing. He couldn't deny that now. He was afraid what was missing had been him. Somewhere along the way, he'd checked out. He'd gotten too comfortable and stopped looking for Shelly, stopped listening, stopped reaching for her.

But maybe—he had to consider this, too—maybe he couldn't ever have been enough. He didn't think bisexuality, if that's what he was supposed to label Shelly's feelings, precluded fidelity, but he didn't really know. Maybe she'd always been unsatisfied, unhappy.

He couldn't help circling back to the fact that, while Shelly had never talked to him about Rachel, she'd clearly talked to Rachel about him. He didn't know if this was a weird comfort, proof she had loved him, or the worst treachery. Either way, it felt awful.

Heartsick. He'd never really understood what it meant until now. Black, fetid mold had seized his life pump, and every throbbing beat sent more sickness pouring through his veins. Every breath only increased the ache coursing through his body.

Finally, Hayden made it home. He pulled into the garage and went in through the side door. In the hallway, he rested his forehead against the closed bedroom door, his palms spread on the warm wood. He stood there until he fell halfway into dreaming, but he didn't turn the knob.

CHAPTER 18

Hayden propped an ankle on his knee, trying to look comfortable in the uncomfortable metal folding chair. Beside him, Rachel perched on the edge of her seat, her hands clenched on her jean-clad thighs. Electricity crackled from her. Hayden felt a weird comfort in the woman's persistent fury. She baffled and enraged him, and he resented and begrudged her, but there was consistency in her passion that reassured him. Rachel Lundgren would never fade away. She wouldn't quietly disintegrate from her own hours. No one would ever roll over in bed and find only her shadow in the sheets beside them. Rachel didn't exist; she burned. And whether he liked it or not, there was warmth in those flames.

Hayden had been quickly introduced to everyone in their row. Sage and Valkyrie were there, and Hayden thought they seemed slightly less wary of him. Melodie introduced him to her parents, a non-assuming couple who nonetheless looked completely at home, as if a lifetime of HOA and PTA meetings had perfectly prepared them for community activism on behalf of their daughter. Mateo sat next to Rachel, his defiant sprawl unapologetic. His face was still a swollen mass of ugly purples and greens and yellows, and Hayden hoped the rest of the people in the room would be unable to look away from this consequence of their casually tolerated contempt.

Valkyrie's knees started bouncing as soon as she eased into her seat beside Hayden. On her other side, Sage rested a hand on her thigh, and Valkyrie stilled, her breath slowing. Hayden couldn't help noticing that neither had family present.

The room was already filling up, and the meeting wasn't supposed to start for another half-hour. News cameras from local stations lined the side walls. Several rows of people near the front sat with Bibles propped on their laps or clutched to their chests. Heads bobbed and whispers whipped and hissed through the air. Rachel had pointed out a handful of community leaders, social workers, and schoolteachers, as well as a few teenagers from the support group, who were seated nearby, but Hayden suspected their group was sadly outnumbered. It was an unfortunate irony; people whose marginalization forced them to fear for their physical safety might be reluctant to step out in a crowd of hostile strangers and cameras to plead their case.

Rachel's lips were pressed firmly shut. He wondered what she was going to say. He'd made a cursory effort last night at hunting down statistics to cite but then decided he had no authority, anyway. He wasn't showing up as some sort of expert, or even as a well-informed advocate. He was just a businessman, a member of the community, who didn't think how a person defined themselves should endanger their lives. He didn't imagine his opinion would have much impact, but at least when those Bible-thumpers stood up and said *not in my neighborhood*, he could let them know it was his neighborhood, too.

He wished he'd asked Lorne to come. Why hadn't he thought of that? Lorne already knew way more about this subject than he did. In fact, the input of schoolteachers should be crucial to the discussion. They saw the impact of homelessness and the restriction of resources on transgender kids all the time. Teachers fought to keep transgender kids present and engaged in the classroom and then sent them out every afternoon into countless unpredictable hazards. Finding a hot meal and a safe place to sleep wouldn't solve their problems, but it would at least provide a solid platform.

Unsurprisingly, the city council addressed the issue of homeless shelters last. A sour-faced woman in big, black glasses read the proposed ordinance. Hayden got lost halfway through the jargon but picked up on the gist: the city council wanted to dispense with federal funding so they could impose whatever housing restrictions they wanted, including a requirement for potential clients to be housed with the gender they had been identified as at birth. Determined, of course, by mandatory strip searches, though this wasn't spelled out.

Microphones were set up on either side of the room between the aisles. Hayden got up and shuffled behind Rachel to join the line for opponents of the measure. Surprisingly, there were almost as many people in that. Most held sheets of paper and read prepared statements with stumbling voices and shaking hands. A few were so polished and loquacious, Hayden suspected they were either running for office or planning on passing a plate.

As the two lines shambled forward, speakers were given two minutes each. He didn't hear a single argument not founded on fear or hatred or put down as God's judgment. Did anyone else see the irony of all the men suddenly compelled to defend already victimized women against the imagined threats of other transgender women? How many had ever waved signs condemning wife-beaters or filed complaints against the handsy guy in their office? Suddenly, these men were heroes standing up for the rights of women.

If they cared as much about the rights and security of women as they claimed, Hayden figured there wouldn't be half as many women who found themselves with nowhere to live but the streets anyway.

From the against column, the speakers ran the gamut. Some were emotional appeals to peace, love, and acceptance. Some, like Mateo's, were personal accounts. The most effective, Hayden thought, were those who came armed with the specifics that had so overwhelmed him last night. Professionals and teachers pointed out that not only were transgender people far more likely to be victims than predators, but most shelters could also not report a single instance of someone using a false claim of transgender identity to attempt to access prey, much less actually succeeding. He listened to people with calm, earnest voices detailing policies and facility designs that ensured safety and protection to everyone, regardless of identity or past trauma. With each person who took their turn, Hayden felt more and more ill-equipped to say anything at all. His palms sweated.

Too soon, Rachel stood at the microphone. Too soon, and too late for him. He tried not to focus on how weird his arms felt dangling at his sides as he listened to her speak in a clear, compelling voice.

"My name is Rachel Lundgren. I'm the owner of Rachel's Blooming Bouquets. My friend Shelly brought this issue home for me when she offered beds to people who had nowhere safe to sleep. I was stunned to learn of the discrimination practiced in our town. We are asked to believe and accept that love for God requires some to force other human beings into unsafe and wretched living situations based on the dimensions of a flap of skin. Some dictate how others will live and do everything in their power to ensure they can't live at all—withhold food, employment, and shelter. But I don't remember Jesus vetting the crowds when he multiplied the bread and the fishes. Jesus fed them all.

"What Jesus would do, though, is beside the point. Some of you so-called faith-based missionaries seem to base your opinions on the behavior of people rather than the grace of God. I am here to oppose discrimination against transgender people in shelters run by the city. The government's responsibility is to care for all citizens equally, not to elevate the political or theological concerns of any one group over the existence and identity of the individual."

Wow. Hayden would have never guessed the fiery Rachel

could be so eloquent. Or that she knew Bible stories. This was not helping his own nerves any. Hearing Rachel combat all this hostility so capably and apparently without a bit of stage fright made him painfully aware of his own insufficiency. Best not to pretend to be more than he was. It wasn't like he was going to change anyone's mind. He shoved his hands into his pockets and leaned toward the microphone.

"My name is Hayden Hill. I'm the owner of Hill Landscaping and Garden Design. Shelly—Shelly Hill—was my wife, and I guess she's the one who brought this home for me, too, although I didn't learn about her involvement until after her death." He was amazed that the words *after her death* dropped off his tongue, as if they weren't the hardest words he'd ever had to say.

"Shelly wasn't a political person. She was a practical person. She focused on results more than whys and wherefores. I'm trying to be more like her, because I'll be honest – there are a lot of why questions I can't answer. But I can look at the results. One side of this room wants solutions that will keep kids alive – keep them off the streets and out of the suicide statistics. One side of this room wants to look in their underwear. For me, the choice is clear. I want kids alive. I want people with nowhere to go to have a place to go. The pronouns they use don't hurt me. But some of the cruelty and callousness I see here does. I'm asking you to be like Shelly, to put compassion over ideology. To figure out how to make this work instead of making excuses for why it can't."

He squeezed past the people still in line and sank back into his seat. His hands were shaking when he laid them on his thighs. He nearly jumped out of his skin when Rachel covered one of them with her own for a moment.

"You did good," she whispered, her eyes on the next speaker.

Melodie spoke, as did her parents. Sage stayed in their seat, but Valkyrie took her turn at the microphone, too. Hayden blinked away tears as the girl he knew only as a bundle of fears and nerves hugged her elbows and spoke her truth in a shaking voice. She was a brilliant little fire poppy, he thought, blooming furiously in the face of flames trying to consume her.

All in all, there were many speakers on both sides. Hayden wondered if the council members had been prepared for the level of community engagement on the issue. How closely were they listening? Would any of the arguments and data and statistics matter in the end, or had their vote been predetermined from the beginning? Hayden glanced around at the reporters and camera people. Even if the council members were unreachable, the public wasn't. And if the community made clear what they wanted, surely the council would vote accordingly.

This small town, though, was historically conservative. They still argued regularly about whether science teachers could discuss evolution in public schools. Some of the restaurants and shops on the nostalgic main street had been asked to take down signs dictating which doors Black people could enter and where they could sit only a few decades ago. Non-churchgoers like Hayden and Shelly were looked askance by their neighbors when they wandered out pajama-clad into the front garden with a beer on a Sunday afternoon. But Hayden knew there was more to the people here than the bumper stickers and ballcaps they wore. Compassion ran deeper than dogma. Didn't it?

"Thank you all for your comments," said the woman with the gavel drily, without a modicum of gratitude in her tone. "We will vote on the ordinance next week. This meeting is concluded."

CHAPTER 19

The weekend was only a day away, but it felt like a year. Hayden's life was an odd paradox. Every minute grated interminably on his senses, like sand on eyeballs. But when he tried later to remember a single detail—what he'd done onsite, what Alex or Jason or one of the guys had said—it faded into a gray amalgamation with no clear edges. Life was inescapable, and at the same time, impossible to grasp.

Hayden didn't know what would become of him when winter arrived. For now, he had planting to do, beds to tend, leaves to rake. The sky was still full of color, and the garden ensconced him in its warm, telluric embrace. The fragrance of the soil still soothed the aching of his throat.

But soon, all would be gray and brown. Cold would moat the house for the season of death, Shelly's ashes would lie frost-covered in the icy earth, and even the oak tree would sleep.

He, though, would have to remain among the conscious. Somehow.

By the time the sun came up Saturday morning, he had already been lying awake for at least an hour. Nothing in the insistent prodding of the sunlight on his eyelids provoked him to open them. He lay there, unwilling to force his limbs into motion, unwilling to fold up the recliner and toss aside the blanket, until the urge to urinate became too great to ignore.

Every muscle in his body ached—the consequence of lying too long in a lumpy chair. He had dozed off, but probably not more than a half-hour at a time. Then came the stillness, the loneliness, the emptiness. Until another doze finally overtook him.

He folded the blanket as if it mattered and drew the curtains, cursing softly at the cheery blare of midmorning light. He stood a long time at the window, looking without seeing.

Somehow, the whole week had been building toward this morning. He couldn't avoid her any longer. The bedroom door pulled him more strongly than any black hole. As he turned the doorknob, he said her name softly. A prayer, a penitence for his earlier trespass.

The unmade bed stood an affront to the weeks since that day she died. How could it not have changed? The folds of the sheet, the bunched-up coverlet, exactly as she had tossed them aside.

He drifted over to stand on her side of the bed. Drifted, because he couldn't feel his feet. There, on the fitted sheet, the indent of her body where she had last slept. Hayden ached with the longing to curl into that spot, to hug close the sheets that had rested on her shoulders, to lie in the impressed curve and feel her warmth seep into his own flesh and bones. But once he lay down in that bed, this ghost sleeper would rise, never to rest there again.

With an unsteady finger, he traced her outline.

"Shelly."

Did her perfume linger in the air, or was that his imagination? Somehow, the room felt like her. Breathed like her.

Already, the space had taken on neglect. Dust silvered the dressers and hung golden in shafts of sunlight. The curtains still stood open around the French doors leading to the backyard. He went to the walk-in closet Shelly had completely overgrown years before. The space he'd ravaged in his fury. Before his wardrobe had been relegated to the spare room, he'd scrunched all his clothes into the corner so she could hang up her dresses and skirts, blouses and sweaters, without fear of wrinkles. Now, the empty rods and blank spaces silently condemned him. Gaping shelves glared where Shelly's purses had once lined the shelves.

Hayden switched on the light and caught sight of himself in the full-length mirror beside the closet. He looked a specter himself, like a man fading away. He leaned forward, staring stupidly into his own dark eyes as if Shelly's reflection might appear if he only gazed long enough. But all he saw was his own hollow face trapped in the black abyss of his pupils, the branches and roots of his iris, the bloodshot traverses of his whites.

He sank down against the wall. There, behind a suitcase, he caught sight of something he'd missed in his whirlwind of eradication. Just one shoe. Hands trembling, heart leaping, he reached for the mate-less sneaker from the dingy, worn-down pair she wore on evening walks and park strolls. Unlike her many perfectly matched loafers and kitten heels and ankle boots, these shoes were worn in. The white was nearly gray, the pink glitter accents all but scrubbed away.

He'd teased her about these shoes when she bought them, asked if there wasn't an age limit on glitter. When one of said shoes went airborne in his direction, he hastily backed down. After that, she'd made a point of adding glitter wherever she could—her ballcap, her light autumn gloves. The sticker on her home laptop.

At work, she had a strictly professional image to maintain, of course. Finance being such a boys' club, the last thing she could afford was any bit of whimsy in her persona there. She'd trusted him with the parts of herself she had to keep hidden so many other places. He'd seen but disregarded it. And then there'd been the part of herself she kept hidden from him, too.

No more late-night walks through the neighborhood park. No more evenings sitting on the bench while he worked in the garden, her ankles crossed, her fingers dangling a sunset-lit glass of burgundy wine. No more Saturday breakfasts at the corner café. No more Sunday afternoons wielding the hose as he washed the truck. He'd never known where he'd find these shoes—drying out on the front walk, tumbled by the garage door, waiting patiently on the back patio.

He wanted to see Shelly. Wanted to look her in the eyes and ask her why, ask her how long, ask her if she'd still loved him, if she'd ever really loved him, if he'd always been a fool. Wanted to tell her how much he loved her, how sorry he was. Wanted to hear her voice, to watch her smile, to feel even the coldest brush of her hand on his skin.

He wanted to talk to her. To rail at her. To listen to her.

But the room was empty, silent, and still. Not so much as a sheet stirred. Unwillingly his mind returned to another room, just as empty, silent, and still as this one.

When he'd seen her lying there on the cold hospital bed, still bearing the marks of attempted resuscitation, he'd known she was gone. Gone as if she'd been away for years. Her absence was stunning and complete. Now, everywhere he moved, he felt that emptiness beside him, a black hole that followed him from room to room.

Unlike a black hole, though, this abyss did not draw him in. It shut him out. It closed in and wouldn't leave him. He'd tried flinging himself into its aphotic darkness but ran into a concrete wall.

"I don't know how to do this." His words fell back on him like stones. "I don't know how to live without you."

Someone would suggest he pack away the rest of her things. Her vanity with its miscellany of mysterious paints, fragrances, and powders. Her dresser, still full. Her jewelry. Her e-book reader on the nightstand. Her magazines in the bathroom.

But his mind rebelled at the thought. It would be like saying she'd never been here, that the space she'd filled hadn't been hers. He didn't want to fill every corner she'd once claimed. All he really wanted was to dissipate, to evaporate.

His rose was gone. What purpose had the dew after the petals fell? Hayden wished the sun could sear him into oblivion, too.

This emptiness was all he had now. He didn't know how to talk to people. The words that left his mouth sounded like a stranger speaking as he thought only: do you know I'm alone? Do you know my Shelly is dead? Do you know I'm broken, broken, broken beyond repair?

Maybe he was wrong to keep his business afloat. Maybe it was the stupidest thing he could do, forcing himself through the motions of ordinary life when nothing was ordinary, and he was barely alive. Maybe he should sell everything. Find a forest somewhere and disappear.

In the wood, it wouldn't matter how long he lay in the moss and watched the leaves overhead talking to each other through the wind. He could lean against the rough bark of a tree that had stood there for countless human lifetimes and imagine he listened to water coursing through the xylem. He wouldn't need much—a roof and a window and a door and a fire. And he didn't want anything. Wanting was a sensation he hardly remembered.

And yet, something vague stirred restlessly within him. For the past few days, he had wanted to help Mateo. He'd wanted Melodie to feel liked and for Sage and Valkyrie to be safe. He'd even wanted to be with Rachel, to hear her, to hate her, to know this woman who had loved Shelly.

It made no sense at all, but then, nothing much made sense anymore.

He couldn't sell everything and walk into the trees. Shelly was in the backyard, after all. Hayden might not be the most sentimental man, but he couldn't leave his wife's ashes to strangers who might cut down the little oak. He'd already told Lorne to add his own ashes to Shelly's before the inevitable sale of the property. Their remains and the oak whose root-fingers held them close would stay together, no matter what.

He supposed some people would find it sad they had no children to live on after they were gone, but the trees they planted, and the spiraling permutations of life would surpass human generations in the end.

Besides, if he couldn't even bear the thought of tossing Shelly's old magazines and makeup, he certainly couldn't sell the house. Forcing himself through the motions of maintaining his business and his home wasn't something he could avoid. Monday, he would try again.

Creakily, he stood up. He placed her shoe on a shelf and shut off the closet light. He walked back to the bed, to his side this time.

"I'm going to try and sleep here tonight," he said. "I'll try."

The doorbell chimed.

CHAPTER 20

He almost ignored it. He wanted to ignore it. But the doorbell was followed by a wild knocking, and the sound of his brother's voice through the door: "I know you're in there, Hayden! I'll use my key if you don't let us in."

Us. Oh, yay. He'd have to act extra normal if Jaciee was here. He loved his sister-in-law, but he knew better than to give her any reason to worry and start making more effort on his behalf. Being fussed over was damn exhausting.

But when he opened the door, Jaciee didn't look worried about him at all. In fact, it was immediately clear this was not a sympathy visit. His brother and his wife were grinning like fools and hanging onto each other like a pair of drunks on an icy boardwalk. Hayden opened his mouth but didn't get a word out.

"Hayden! You gotta come out with us. We're celebrating."

"Celebrating?"

"We're pregnant!" Jaciee's words tumbled over his question.

"Oh, wow." Hayden stepped backward, and Jaciee and Lorne followed him into the house. "That's awesome. I'm happy for you."

Lorne's eyes, when they met his, held none of the shadows of their childhood that had haunted him so long. Hayden felt his own cheeks splitting with his brother's infectious joy. He gripped Lorne's shoulder.

"You're gonna be great."

"Obviously."

Hayden pretended not to hear the catch in Lorne's deep voice.

"Let me clean up a little, and we can head out. How far along are you?" Was that a question he was supposed to ask? "Where do you want to go to celebrate?" he hurried on, just in case it wasn't.

Lorne's voice came after him as Hayden headed to the bathroom to brush his teeth and wash his face. "Maybe six weeks? We're not totally sure. And how about Giuseppe's?"

Giuseppe's was their favorite, with a rooftop patio and the best lasagna Hayden had ever eaten. The last time he'd been there was with Shelly. Of course, it was. They'd gone everywhere together.

No, that wasn't right. He took her everywhere, but she'd gone to places without him. All the absences and excursions he'd never questioned because he was content to be left alone at home. Never guessing she had another life entirely. Another love. God, he needed to stop running this same loop in his head.

He wondered if Shelly had ever gone to Giuseppe's with Rachel. His chest ached.

"Sounds good," he called back.

He could hear Jaciee rummaging through his kitchen, doors opening and dishes clanging. He hurried to throw on a nicer shirt and brush his thinning hair with a damp comb. He needed a haircut. Mostly, he needed to get Jaciee out of the house before she got inspired.

The place wasn't exactly a cesspit, but it wasn't clean, either. The refrigerator was a Tupperware wasteland. Was he supposed to return those? Panic swelled briefly. How the heck was he supposed to remember who had brought which container?

The anxiety subsided as quickly as it had risen. He didn't

really care. If they cared that much, they'd have put their names on them.

Why was it that other people's consolation always resulted in more drudgery for those grieving? Dead flowers to be thrown away, useless vases to be washed and stored as if someday, they might have another purpose. Food to be sorted, dishes to be washed and returned. The funeral home had supplied him with Thank-You cards meant to be sent out to everyone who signed the guest book for Shelly's memorial. How was that an expectation people held?

He could barely get dressed in the morning. And suddenly, he was supposed to adopt the sensibilities of a Victorian matron? He didn't think so.

Hayden grabbed a pair of loafers and headed into the kitchen, where Jaciee peered into the refrigerator with an expression of distaste.

"See anything you like?" Hayden asked. "You're welcome to it."

She laughed. "Those all look more like science experiments than food at this point. Want me to clear it out for you?"

"Naw. I got it. Besides, aren't new moms supposed to have delicate stomachs? I may develop morning sickness myself when I start scraping those dishes."

"Good point. I haven't had much trouble with that yet, but why tempt fate?"

Hayden sighed with relief as Jaciee trailed him out of the kitchen and to the front door. She might not be the most domestic creature, but he knew she'd do anything to help. And much as he loved her, the last thing he wanted was another woman bustling around his kitchen and making small talk. He could barely tolerate the voice in his own head.

He thought of Rachel's dragonfly body thrumming with intensity, her sharp tongue. Her gentle fingers, working the plants in the soil. With Rachel, all talk was big talk. But still, somehow, she had a gift for life. Like a briar, dense with massive thorns and tangled branches, harsh and forbidding to interlopers, but refuge and habitat for countless creatures.

Hayden shook his head. He had to stop thinking about her. About *it*.

"Should I take the truck?" he offered.

"No, I'll drive us," his brother said.

Outside, Hayden climbed into the back seat of their Outback, considering for the first time that Lorne and Jaciee had been planning to be parents since before they first bought this car together.

How long had they been married? He wasn't sure. Other people's anniversaries had never seemed like a thing to keep track of. Six years? Seven? Unlike him, Lorne had taken his time settling down.

Hayden didn't try to force conversation, content to sit back and let Jaciee and Lorne's voices wash over him. He looked at the back of Jaciee's head and wondered if she would ever do to Lorne what Shelly had done to him. Would waiting as long as they had to get married insure them somehow against his own failure? Would having a child draw them closer together or drive them apart, year by year?

Was every relationship doomed to either collapse or betrayal? Maybe some of those obnoxious talking heads were right, and there was a biological shelf-life on monogamy. He'd always thought that sort of claim was specious, a poorly masked attempt to justify selfishness and narcissism.

And he knew better. Plenty of animals and birds mated for life quite successfully. Some didn't even take new mates once their initial partner died. Clearly, there was nothing imperative in human faithlessness.

If he were honest with himself – not that he really wanted to be – maybe he'd never allowed Shelly to be as close of a partner as Jaciee was to Lorne. Maybe part of him had always been afraid she'd see that dirty little trailer park kid inside him and realize how much better than him she was. Now that it was too late, he realized that was as unfair to Shelly as it was to the kid he'd been.

Lorne, he thought, had more faith in Jaciee – he let her all the way in.

No. He and Shelly hadn't been doomed. Shelly hadn't been a victim of biology. She'd simply chosen someone else. Maybe because in some way, he'd allowed her to. And then she'd chosen to lie about it, to act as if nothing had changed. As if she still loved him.

His hands clenched into fists. *Why* was such a stupid question, and he wished to God he could stop asking it, but it ran around and around in his head like a rabid squirrel.

In ten minutes, they were parking at Giuseppe's. Hayden did his best to pull himself out of his head, to join the conversation about nursery schemes and general baby talk. Gooey parmesan garlic bread sticks and red wine made the task easier. Hayden's jaw ached with the effort of smiling and chewing without grinding his teeth. He tried to focus on the joy shining on his brother's face.

Lorne had stood by him through the worst of times. Somehow, he had to stand by Lorne in this, the best of times. Jaciee pretended to accept his efforts at face value, but Hayden caught her looking at him with worry in her eyes.

He was lucky, he tried to convince himself. He had good people, people who loved him, still in his life. And he was about to become an uncle. Someday, eventually, that had to make him a little bit happy, didn't it?

"I just realized there's going to be a little person I can endlessly corrupt with no consequences to myself," he said around a mouthful of lasagna. "There's a lot of possibility here. And I have nine months—well, eight, maybe—to plan."

"I'd rethink that 'no consequences' if I were you," Jaciee said, kicking him under the table.

He grinned. "Plausible deniability will be the key, I think."

"Beggars can't be choosers when it comes to babysitters," Lorne said cheerfully. "We'll have to take our chances."

"Whoa, wait. Did I say I would babysit?"

"Sorry, dude. Comes with the territory. Non-negotiable."

"I can help you baby-proof the house," Jaciee offered brightly.

"Oh, no."

"Oh, yes."

Hayden stole the last breadstick without an ounce of remorse. Almost, almost, he felt good.

CHAPTER 21

In the end, Hayden still couldn't do it. Couldn't bring himself to climb into the bed that would always be empty of Shelly. He didn't want to rid the house of her last impressions, to erase the shape of her body from the mattress, to calm the wake of her rising from the crumpled sheets. He didn't want to lie in the dark and not hear her soft snoring, not feel the heat of her body beside him.

He'd intended to do it. Surely, that had to count for something. Some kind of progress. Though, he wasn't sure why progress was a goal. Why was moving further away from his wife supposed to be a good thing? He already felt he was moving too fast, as if life were a river, and he'd left Shelly stranded on a sandbar somewhere. He was caught up in a wild current and had to fight to keep his eyes on her silhouette, which grew smaller and smaller every day. Try as he might, even treading water wasn't possible.

Eventually, she'd disappear altogether.

No.

He wrapped the blanket around himself as he staggered out of the chair instead of folding it up. Already, the mornings were significantly chillier. He made it to the kitchen and hit the button on the coffeemaker.

Jaciee had said much to him since the day that split his life into with-Shelly and without-Shelly, but the most important involved coffee. They'd stood in the kitchen after the funeral.

"Here," she'd said, firmly but kindly. "You need to set up the coffeemaker for tomorrow morning."

"What?"

"Make the coffee, Hayden."

He'd raised his bleary gaze to the tub of coffee grounds, a box of filters, and a spoon. The coffee pot stood open. Lacking the energy to argue, he'd begun the process by rote.

"You need to do this every night," Jaciee said. "Every night, okay? Promise me."

"I promise."

At the time, he hadn't understood. But Hayden Hill was almost inexorably a man of his word and after given his promise, he couldn't go back on it. So, every night, no matter how tired—or sometimes, how drunk—he was, he dutifully poured the cold water and scooped the coffee.

And every morning, when he pushed the little red button and listened to the reluctant creaks and groans of the tired old percolator, he knew he'd done something. Won something. Pushed back against the oblivion and held his place sovereign, if only for a moment. He should tell her she'd been right. Jaciee liked to hear she was right.

He poured this morning's brew into a tumbler that would withstand the frosty air and stepped through the back door. Even with the blanket slung around his shoulders, he shivered. He'd shoved his feet into a pair of slippers, but with no socks, his ankles felt like ice.

He walked across the backyard to the patio that opened from the master bedroom. Pulling the blanket tight, he sank down against the French doors. He sipped the coffee—hot, bitter, and bracing.

If he didn't look back over his shoulder, he could imagine Shelly on the other side of the doors behind him. Her hand pressed on the glass. Her gaze following his own through the dying garden.

Because it was dying in earnest now. Even so, Hayden couldn't begrudge the heavy frost that had doomed the last of the late summer flowers. Caught in this brief eternity between day and night, the frost crystals glistened and shone in the dawn that would soon destroy them. They glittered like diamonds set in gold, outlining each curling leaf, each withered petal, each bent stalk in glory far exceeding the ebullience of their freshest, wildest blooms. In a few minutes, though, all that beauty would evaporate as if it had never been. All that would remain would be decaying beds of spent flowers and drooping grass.

The air was hushed and still, but soon, the wind would blow. And when it did, the heavily jeweled leaves of the spreading trees would fall, surrendering their hold on sleeping limbs. The yard would be full of the susurrating shifting and sifting of piles of leaves as they rushed from one corner to another, tumbling over each other and tugging on every flower and stalk in their path.

Shelly's tree was different. This was one of many reasons he'd been set on an oak for her headstone. Unlike other trees, whose leaves let go suddenly and easily, the oak would keep its leaves all the long, cold, dark winter months. When every other tree stood bare-limbed and absent any reminder of life, the oak's dry, brown leaves would wave like banners in the wind. Little silhouettes of promise against the bleakest skies. Not until the new growth forced its way out next spring would the old leaves fall, their commission fulfilled.

The coffee warmed his throat and his hands, but his ass was cold on the concrete. Ironic, those oak leaves. He'd wanted something that held on, something that didn't give up in even the fiercest winter. But it looked like Shelly had let go of their marriage a long time ago; somehow, he hadn't noticed.

If she were really on the other side of those doors, she wouldn't be looking in the same direction. She'd be over at the window, instead, affixing tiny messages to the leg of a homing pigeon bound for Rachel's house.

But she wasn't there. If anything, she was deep in the heart of that oak tree, perhaps thrumming through the mycorrhizal fungi cobwebbing the soil underground. He took a grim and bitter satisfaction knowing that if she couldn't haunt him, she couldn't haunt Rachel, either. They were both bereft. Both lacking her presence.

Come spring, Shelly would be in the pale green buds, in the creeping pill bugs and fluttering butterflies. In the new ring of growth forming underneath the spreading bark. Even in the pollen-heavy breezes dancing bloom-to-bloom and gusting through the open windows.

Maybe Hayden did have more of Shelly than Rachel did, but now, he realized he'd only ever possessed a thread of her soul. Everywhere, he found frayed bits of colors he hadn't known were hers.

Cold. He was cold to his damn bones.

People weren't static, after all. They were more like kaleidoscopes. The colors, the shapes, stayed the same, but every shift, every turn, brought new shimmering patterns, and how different they looked in the light than in the dark of night.

Hayden hadn't needed to know every one of the innumerable shapes Shelly might take. But he had believed that he could hold those multicolored sequins of her soul in his hand, and somehow, they would all, always, fit in his palm. No matter their iteration.

But at least one sequin had fallen free. How many others?

He pushed himself off the concrete with a grunt. His knees cracked. What was he, seventy? He scooped up his coffee and hobbled over to the deck to return to the warmth of the quiet house. Wearily, he wished he could quit replaying these questions in his head. Maybe he'd never make sense of this, maybe it would never fit into a neat window box in his head, and still he couldn't seem to stop trying to link up edges that didn't fit.

In his pocket, his phone buzzed. A text from Melodie. She

asked if he was coming to the shop and added that Rachel wouldn't be in today or tomorrow.

It was nice of her to let him know he could avoid awkward encounters with his wife's mistress, but he didn't really want anything to do with Blooming Bouquets.

He couldn't blame Melodie for being confused about his interest, or the extent of his involvement. He was confused as heck himself.

This must be why death literature said not to make any major financial or living decisions the first year following a loss. Hayden couldn't figure out what he wanted from one minute to the next, much less stick to it. Probably because he mostly didn't want anything, except for Shelly back.

What if he could have her back, right this minute, but he had to accept her affair with Rachel, too?

Damn it. Why was he torturing himself? She wasn't coming back because she wasn't anywhere. She just wasn't.

Maybe it wasn't even right to think of Shelly as his wife anymore. It had been *till death do us part*, hadn't it? Whatever identity Shelly held now, whether cell or soul or soil, it was free of him. Free of any encumbrances. Free.

Tears unexpectedly burned his eyes. His wedding ring weighed impossibly heavy on his finger. Maybe Shelly wasn't his wife anymore, but he still felt like her husband. He'd thought they had decades left. He wasn't ready for this. He couldn't do it.

Panic clawed at his throat, and he stood rigid, clutching the counter as he gasped for air. His chest spasmed painfully. He closed his eyes and fought to count, to control his breathing, to push out the agony with an oblivion made up of the sound of his blood rushing in his ears and air whistling between his pursed lips. Long moments passed, his sentience returning as the adrenaline dump left him dizzy.

Melodie. What had Melodie been saying? He clung to his phone, rereading the messages as if they were brand new. He typed out a reply with shaking fingers.

Maybe if I rescue any tomatoes, I'll bring you some salsa. How hot do you like it?

Somewhere between Tibet and New Mexico, but not as mild as Texas.

Hayden laughed weakly.

I'll see what I can do.

He didn't want to go back to the shop, but he needed to be somewhere. The idea of drifting through the house after working in the garden all day, of being trapped with nothing but the shape of Shelly's absence for company, horrified him. He turned the television on more these days than he ever had when she was alive. He couldn't bear the silence, but the tinned laughter and voices made him lonelier than if he'd been on the moon.

Lorne would drop everything and come over if Hayden asked him to. But his brother wanted things from him. Wanted to know how he was. Wanted to know what he was going to do next. Wanted some reassurance that Hayden wasn't going to fade away somehow. Wanted him to be okay, but Hayden didn't know if he would ever be okay.

Those interminable hours between dusk and dawn. The hour between reaching for Shelly and realizing she wasn't there. Between hearing her step in the hall and knowing it was only the house settling. Between loading the dishwasher "the right way" and remembering it didn't matter anymore. Between waking beside her under heavy eyelids and opening them to the memory of her slack face in a cold room.

Buzz.

A happy face emoji followed by flowers.

Today, at least, he could find a way to endure fewer of those hours.

CHAPTER 22

Hayden's resolve kicked in quickly. Inside, he dressed hurriedly and headed out to the garage.

The wheelie stool, big rope baskets, shears, trowel, gloves, and wheelbarrow. The broad-rimmed sunhat Shelly said made him look like Vincent Van Gogh. He wasn't as pasty as the artist, but probably as hollow-faced, and he'd never been the sort to grow one of those luxuriant Viking beards. His, like Vincent's, was more scruff than shrub after he failed to shave for a few days.

Shelly's teasing had felt companionable, not mean. He'd been so sure of her affection, so certain of his place in her arms. He'd never prickled or taken umbrage when she laughed at him. Now that, like everything else, was an unanswerable question. Had she secretly despised him? Had what he'd thought was good-natured ribbing been the only outlet for her hidden contempt? A sudden repulsion of himself, of his very skin, seized him. God, he hated himself. Hated his brain for tormenting him like this, day after day. Hated his soft belly, his thinning hair, his wiry arms, his big, spreading toes. Hated the sound of his own voice in his head.

The air was still chilly, but Hayden got to work in his shirt sleeves. The sun was shining, and he'd warm up soon. Besides, there was a perverse and inexplicable comfort in physical discomfort amid psychological misery. Maybe it was nothing more than a distraction for the mind, solace taken in concentrating on a pain that could end, a pain that could be managed and controlled, instead of one with no edges or expiration.

Over the past few weeks, he had pruned the flowers and raked the beds, but he'd neglected the vegetables. Nothing he did made sense these days.

He dug up the onions, but they had to go straight to compost. He'd left them in the ground too long, vulnerable to bugs and rot. He wheeled their soft, blackened bodies over to the compost bin and chucked them in. He was suddenly and fiercely glad he'd had Shelly cremated instead of buried in a box.

The tomatoes and peppers were salvageable, but he didn't think they'd last long. Maybe he should just make salsa with all of them. He probably had store-bought onions in the house, although he couldn't remember the last time he'd had reason to look. The cilantro was a little wilted, also; surely the blender would take care of that.

He composted the greens, too. Normally, he and Shelly made weekly or biweekly trips to the local food pantry with whatever produce they couldn't eat, but the thought hadn't even crossed his mind since she'd been gone. One more guilt to carry. He'd never realized, when he'd encountered people after a loss, how much energy grieving took. One regret, shame, and fault, piled up after another.

The next time he went to the food pantry, someone was sure to ask where Shelly was. He'd been so insulated these past days, surrounded by people who knew what had happened. More and more often, he was going to find himself in places where he had to explain that his wife was gone. The butcher's counter at the grocery store. The post office. And the food pantry.

People intent on meaningless pleasantries—*Nice weather today, how have you been, I haven't seen your wife for a while*—weren't prepared for a near-stranger to collapse into tears. Hayden didn't know how he was going to do it.

He could go to a different grocery store. There was another post office on the other side of town. He wondered if there was another food pantry that would take fresh produce. In such a small town, there might not be. And many food pantries only accepted non-perishables. Shelly had made the calls to find this one. It operated out of an Episcopalian church just a few streets over, and once a week, they offered fresh produce to their clients.

Well. He had time to figure it out, didn't he? The garden was done for the year. There would be all the extra jars of salsa, but he could force those on Lorne and the crew at work. Salsa had to be more welcome than those despondent heaps of zucchini and kale that appeared in breakrooms all around the country every autumn. Maybe by next summer, he could face what he couldn't face now. Or maybe the Episcopalians would have new volunteers who wouldn't remember him and Shelly, and no one would ask where she was. That seemed almost worse. Somebody should miss her. She'd been donating through that church for years. They should have noticed she was gone.

The poor, naked stalks of the tomato plants hunched miserably, shorn of their fruit, leaves curling as if they'd tried to wrap themselves up against that frost. Nothing remained of the sparkling crystals now. Even the moisture was rapidly wicked away by the bright sun. The temperatures would be well into the seventies by afternoon.

He touched one pathetic leaf, scraping its withered edge over the pad of his finger. The same stupid question he'd asked himself in the garage rose again for no good reason at all.

What would he rather? Have Shelly back, alive, well, with everything as it had been before? Him ignorant, and her in love with a woman he'd never met. Or live with the truth but without her?

In short: would he rather Shelly be dead than share her? Or—he swallowed—lose her? Surely, it had only been a matter of time before she left, no matter what Rachel claimed. Although Shelly had a mathematical mind, she was—she'd been—a deeply empathetic person. She'd have been sick at the idea of hurting him.

Maybe that wasn't true, either. Shelly was soft-hearted, sure, but maybe he'd fallen outside of her sympathies a long time ago. Maybe she hated him. Loathed him. Didn't care one way or the other how he would feel if he ever found out. Maybe she stayed precisely because she cared so little, because it cost her absolutely nothing to lie to him day after day. Maybe their marriage had become nothing more than a cold calculation of financial security and societal tranquility.

No. He rejected that possibility. Despite everything, he wanted her here. He wanted to see the sunlight on her hair, see the laughter leaping in her eyes. He wanted to lie down in their bed and feel the weight of her body on the mattress beside him. He wanted to fight over the last of the good leftovers. He wanted to pour her a glass of cabernet. He wanted to go to the food pantry with her on Saturdays.

He would choose Shelly, every time. Even if she didn't choose him. He'd choose her.

And maybe it was a new myth he was writing, but he couldn't bring himself to believe that Shelly didn't love him. Maybe she wasn't in love with him; he had to accept that. Surely, a person couldn't be in love with two completely different people at the same time. But that didn't mean she despised him.

His eyes idly followed a sluggish wasp as he catalogued things he knew were true.

She still curled up against him when they watched TV, dangling her legs over his thighs when there was more than enough room on the couch for two. She still kissed him goodbye every morning before she left for the office. Not a peck on the cheek, but a real kiss on the mouth. She still brought him cool glasses of sweet tea while he worked in the garden and listened to his stories from work.

Shelly had loved Rachel. Sour as the words were in his mouth, they tasted true. But she had loved him, too. He couldn't make those things fit together, so he must learn to carry them in separate pockets.

Fiercely, he wished she'd never met Rachel. What sort of foul fate was that at work? If only another florist had opened a shop closer to her office. If only Rachel hadn't taken a job there. If only Hayden had bought her flowers himself.

If only. If only.

Would he have been enough then? She might have found someone else besides Rachel. Or she might have just been miserable, suffering from some emptiness he hadn't noticed. One thing Hayden didn't doubt was that Rachel had been the only one. The fact that she had carried on what was obviously a serious emotional relationship for a year and a half was a weird testament itself to whatever passed for faithfulness in her heart.

This would be so much easier if he could hate her. Could boil with rage at every memory and shout *good riddance* to her name. And sometimes, he did. Mostly, he hated her for being gone, not for cheating. He hated the way he hurt. Hated the way he thought about her, every minute, every day, till the inside of his skull was scraped raw.

One of the brochures from the funeral home talked about anger and the stages of grief. Hayden didn't need anyone's permission to be angry at his dead wife, but he didn't deceive himself into thinking he could live in that anger long. It was nothing more than a stalling tactic, a shoving away of the sadness that would always push its way back in. Anger felt twisty, complicated, like a knot he could eventually untie if he worked it long enough.

Sadness was remarkably simple. It could not be navigated, traversed, or summitted. It could not be untied. Sadness was. Is. Will be.

Hayden thought the stages-of-grief talk was nonsense, anyway. It looked so neat, laid out there on paper. Finish one, then work your way through the other. Check, check, check. It might take a couple of times through, but healing was assured at the finish line. He thought the construct existed more for observers of mourning than for the mourners themselves. People craved a box, so they could close the flaps, seal the edges, and store grief away out of sight. They could just point to the brightly painted arrows on the ground and direct you to the next square.

The spurt of energy that had propelled Hayden through his harvest had evaporated with the frost. Lifting his body to a standing position was like lifting a boulder. Wearily, he replaced all his tools.

Inside, he looked longingly at the recliner as he passed by, but he stayed on his feet. If he sat down, he might not get up again until tomorrow.

Salsa. He'd promised Melodie salsa. Who knew salsa could be a reason for living?

He washed the vegetables and dried them on clean towels. Dug out the blender and got down all the Mason jars from the top shelf of the pantry. He tossed rough chopped vegetables and cilantro around the blades, added a dash of lime juice and a few shakes of salt, and started the motor. The scream of the blender oddly soothed him, driving out the voices in his head. He lost himself in the rhythm—chop, toss, blend, pour. He lost track of how many batches it took to use up all the produce and was sorry to be done.

Twenty-two jars of salsa. Digging through the junk drawer, he fished out a mostly-still-good Sharpie and wrote the date on each lid. He set one aside for Melodie and hesitated. Should he take one for the kids in the storeroom? One for Rachel?

He grimaced. Was he really debating whether to take a jar of homemade salsa to his wife's mistress?

Nonetheless, when he headed out the door a few minutes later, three jars of salsa clanged together in the cloth bag slung over his shoulder.

CHAPTER 23

Melodie smiled broadly as Hayden walked through the chiming door.

"I'd almost given up on you."

"I ran by the store for chips." Hayden lifted the two bags he carried. "I hope you like your salsa spicy."

Melodie laughed and waggled her eyebrows dramatically.

Hayden felt something tight inside him unwind, just a little. It had been a while since he'd had anything to offer anyone else. "I brought extra for everyone."

"Oh, they'll love that. It'll be a while before anyone shows up, but I'll put the stuff back there with a note letting them know it's from you."

"Thanks. There's—there's some for Rachel, too."

"Sure." As Melodie took the bags from him, her gaze slid discreetly away. "I'll leave it here behind the counter with her name on it. Otherwise, there might not be any left by morning."

The shop was empty and outside, evening shadows crept down the sidewalks. Sunday evenings probably weren't busy at the flower shop.

"I was thinking," he began, although, he hadn't been thinking about it at all and had no idea the words were coming out of his mouth until he heard them emerge, "maybe you could walk down to the store with me and help me pick out a bouquet after you close up here."

Melodie's eyes rounded in surprise. "I thought you and Rachel both hated cut flowers. That's kind of the whole point of Blooming Bouquets."

"I know. I do. But Shelly loved them. I never knew that before. The regular florist is closed now, but I thought I could pick out some flowers at the grocery store and put them under her oak tree. That's where her ashes are—under an oak in our backyard."

"I'd be honored to help you pick out something pretty for her. I'll be ready to close in about ten minutes."

"Perfect."

The florist section of the grocery store was awful, of course. Buckets of forlorn blooms under fluorescent lights, interspersed with tiny, tight-to-bursting mylar balloons on plastic sticks. Shelves of overpriced vases and rolls of tissue paper stood behind the counter. Tiny rectangular cards and little packets of flower food were displayed under a sign that read "Take One."

Hayden must have been making a face because Melodie chuckled when she peeked at him.

"Don't overthink it," she said. "We're just looking for pretty flowers that smell good. Not planting a garden or changing the world."

"Thank God. Don't think I'd have too much chance at the latter, at least."

Melodie shrugged. "Sometimes it's the little things. But we're here for Shelly tonight. Do you know her favorite flower?"

Hayden stilled. He should know that. Of all people in the world, he should know that.

Had he really been this self-consumed? His entire life was devoted to plants and the living world. He easily spent hours a day thinking about flowers. How could he not know which ones were his wife's favorite? Frantically, he scoured his memories for clues. She loved the scent of lilacs in the spring, he knew. She had insisted he plant red dahlias in the back garden every year and a strip of bright-faced marigolds along the front walk. But that was as much to deter ants as anything else.

Melodie saw the look on his face. "What about her favorite color?"

He seized on that. "Blue."

"Naturally. The color least likely to be found in cut flowers! But we'll make it work."

Melodie took her time, strolling around and around the buckets of flowers and peering through the glass doors of a refrigerated case. She managed to find some rather unnatural-looking blue carnations. She augmented these with hues of pale pink and violet and white and filled the whole thing in with several sprigs of baby's breath, so the overall illusion was almost of a spectrum of blue. She handed the armful of stems to Hayden.

"Thank you. It's lovely." He was surprised that he meant it. "You have an eye for arrangements. Did you work at a traditional florist shop before you came to Blooming Bouquets?"

"Nope, I just love flowers."

Hayden had to convince the clerk he didn't want a vase, and he didn't want any tissue paper, just a bit of hemp string to hold it all together. It took some doing, but he prevailed. An idea seized him, and he spoke before he could overthink it.

"Would you – would you like to see Shelly's tree? I totally understand if that's too weird. Or too much."

Melodie's face softened, and she took his hand. Her palms felt warm and strong. Not for the first time, he thought she seemed much older than her years. "I'd love that."

"Do you want to follow me to the house in your car? If you're not comfortable doing that, I can drive you back over here when you're ready to go home."

"I'm fine with following you. But maybe give me the address, too, in case you lose me. I'm not much of a speed-demon."

The world was fully dark by the time their two cars pulled into the driveway. Hayden experienced a spasm of apprehension.

He hoped Melodie didn't feel weird about being alone at the house of what was practically a strange man. He decided to lead her through the back gate instead of through the house.

She followed closely behind him on the flagstone path. The garden was a gradient of shadows. A sickle moon hung low in the sky, and the streetlight lent some faint definition.

"Wait here," said Hayden. "I'll get us some light."

He always left the back doors unlocked. Probably not smart, but there had to be some advantages to living in a small town, and he'd never had reason to regret it. Not yet anyway. He reached inside and switched on the fairy lights strung through the backyard. The addition had been all Shelly, something she'd found on Pinterest.

"Ooh," Melodie breathed. "How pretty."

She spun slowly, looking around. The fountain still burbled, though he'd probably shut off the water in the next week. It didn't freeze often, but it wasn't worth the risk. Tonight, though, the melodious sound of the falling water brought serenity to the yard. Now that the lights were on, the winding course of the stone path was revealed, the broad enormity of the spreading beech, the many alcoves of shrubs.

"It was prettier a week ago," he said. "I've torn out the vegetables and the annual flowers and cut back my perennials. It's honestly quite stripped bare now. Soon, it will be full of leaves." He gestured to the beech, its night-black limbs heavy with scarlet.

"Yeah, no doubt. That beast looks like it sheds a ton of leaves."

"It does. But it's worth it. Beeches are wonderful old trees. Their autumn color is gorgeous. And although they compete in the forest, beeches and oaks are common companions. Shelly's tree is near the back fence. Gotta give these two giants their space."

Melodie carried the bouquet of flowers. In the false electric light, the little oak seemed even more upstart than usual, its awkward, skinny limbs sharp and black, its russet leaves fluttering like rebel banners.

"I planted it for her," he said, "so it's only a teenager now. But one day, it'll be massive like the beech. Oaks are slow growers but long-lived. Kind of the opposite of Shelly, I guess. She always seemed older than her years when we were kids. So serious and stable. But she didn't last long."

Gently, Melodie laid the immense bouquet against the narrow trunk. Together they stood in the moonlight, staring at the silvered blooms. They'd be wilted by morning, without water, and with the frost coming.

That's why I hate them, he wanted to shout. *Because they die. They die and do absolutely nothing but look beautiful.*

But something in them had spoken to Shelly in ways he hadn't understood. Every week, she'd chosen a vase of fresh blooms that died before her eyes.

Hayden wanted to make sense of that. He wanted a moment, a mere breath, to be enough in and of itself.

But it wasn't. His hands fisted. It hadn't been enough. They hadn't had long enough.

Melodie's voice broke the silence. "She would have loved knowing you were keeping her here with you. Part of your garden, carried up through the arms of the oak tree into the sky."

Hayden turned to stare at Melodie. Somehow, this young person had understood exactly what he'd been thinking when he'd buried Shelly's ashes among the roots of the oak.

"Why are you so nice to me?" he asked abruptly.

Melodie blinked, her eyes flashing white. "Shelly loved you. And you loved Shelly. Why wouldn't I be nice to you?"

"Do you really believe that? That she loved me?"

"I know she did. She talked about you all the time. I think, in some ways, Blooming Bouquets was as much about you as it was about Rachel."

"How is that possible?" Hayden didn't know why he was asking this virtual child these questions, but he had nowhere else to go.

Melodie shrugged. "I don't know. People are complicated.

And weird. But I know she did love you. And she thought about you when she was in the shop. She didn't do much as far as the plants—she was more a numbers girl. But she would say things about how much you liked this plant or the other. Or how annoyed you would be by the customers who came in looking for cut flowers."

Hayden smiled weakly as she laughed. "I guess she was right about that."

"And besides, you've always been nice to me."

"Have I?" Hayden wasn't so sure.

"Well, you might have been a little out of your depth when you first showed up, but you're a fast learner. You helped Mateo. And you spoke up for all of us at the meeting the other night. Nobody gets it right all the time. But you're someone who tries. I see why Shelly needed you so much."

The words were more balm than they should have been. Hayden told himself Melodie was being kind and saying whatever she thought would make him feel better, which was almost certainly true, but hell. He wanted to believe her.

Maybe what she said about Shelly was even true. After all, she'd known a Shelly he didn't realize existed. A Shelly who lied to her husband but not to her mistress, he reminded himself.

There was something he needed to piece out. Was that the whole appeal of an affair? Having someone she could be honest and ugly and uncovered with? When had he stopped being that person?

It wasn't only the relationship with Rachel, but this whole new world of hers—the shop, the kids, the storeroom. A world that held no space for him.

Only, somehow, it did, didn't it? He was here now, after all. While it felt uncomfortable, it was a good sort of discomfort, like fitting into a new pair of jeans. Everything was somehow part of his story now. He kept telling himself he could walk away from them—that he would walk away from them—but he wasn't sure that was true.

"You're a kind person, Melodie," he said. "You deserve good things."

She smiled brightly. "Thanks. I think so, too. Hug?"

As she wrapped him in a quick, warm embrace, Hayden silently confessed he was coming to crave the physical connections people around him insisted on offering. All the time, he was drowning. A hug or a hand on his arm was a lifeline, a rope thrown in a storm. Hayden hadn't known a person could be so starved for touch. He forced himself not to hang on as she pulled back.

"Thanks for letting me be part of this," she said. "I'd love to see the garden in the daylight sometime."

"You'll have to come back in the spring. It's not much to look at now. But it's beautiful when everything blooms. Maybe everyone can come over. We'll barbecue, or whatever it is normal people do."

"That'd be awesome."

As the sound of her car pulling away faded into the night, Hayden shut off the fairy lights. They were too pretty, too bright, too much of a lie. His garden was a graveyard now.

He crouched down beside the flowers, shivering a little in the cold autumn air, and pressed his palm to the soil. He could feel every grain of dirt, every tiny pebble, against his skin. The infinitesimal churning of earthworms and pill bugs and ants. But he couldn't feel Shelly.

CHAPTER 24

Hayden left the lights off as he moved through the house. He could probably have navigated the rooms in complete darkness, but there was no need: faint illumination from the streetlight silvered through the curtains and picked out the edges of furniture and doorways. A sense of unreality bubbled around him.

He thought of the flowers lying out there in the chilly night, their petals already curling up against the chill, their stalks shutting down, giving up, surrendering to the death they'd been resisting since they were cut. They would find no reprieve now.

The bedroom door slid open over the carpet with a sound like a drawn breath. Hayden stripped slowly, every movement taking on the sensation of ritual. He didn't want anything between his skin and the sheets tonight.

He stood by the edge of the bed for a long moment. He wasn't sure why he was waiting. No matter how long he stood there, the bed would never be less empty. He couldn't make any new memories with Shelly. They'd never try a new food together or travel somewhere they hadn't been before or giggle at a movie theatre. The only memories now would be of the firsts without—the first birthday, the first Christmas, the first new restaurant he wouldn't share with her. The first time he slept in a bed empty of her.

They'd slept apart plenty of times, of course. There'd been trips away, nights when one or the other was up all night on the couch with the sniffles. But the bed was still hers, even when she wasn't there. Now the bed was his, only his.

One flick of his wrist, and the impromptu sculpture of sheets she hadn't known she was making on her last morning was destroyed. Hayden threw his leg onto the mattress and climbed in, the motion awkward and difficult, like he'd forgotten how to get into a bed. He lay down on the cold, fitted sheet and pulled the blankets over his bare flesh. The fabric settled over him, the springs and foam under his weight cushioning and holding him. He was suddenly aware of every ache, every strain he'd gotten sleeping in the recliner. The comfort was a cruel blow, a sort of betrayal. How could anything feel good?

Bodies go on and on, while even dead flowers go to seed.

He curled over onto his side and reached across, resting his hand on Shelly's pillow. If she were here, his arm would be slung across her breasts, his fingers on her cheek perhaps, or along the curve of her neck. He closed his eyes and tried to summon up a visceral memory of her body under his touch. The soft warmth of her skin, the rising and falling of her chest, the feather touch of her hair. He might stroke his thumb over her bottom lip. Might cup her bare shoulder in his palm, nudge her thighs with his knee. He might hear her low laugh.

But his mind failed him. His arm lay heavy and flat. The room was still and silent, undisturbed by the whirring of the ceiling fan Shelly always turned on before going to bed. There was no magic here. No mystery. No ghost.

He rolled over onto her side of the bed, burrowing his face in her pillow and breathing in the faint scent of her shampoo. At least, that was what he told himself. He wasn't sure he smelled anything at all. But God, he wanted to. The thought that every sensory memory of his wife was already lost was too awful to bear.

He curled into himself, holding his knees tightly against his belly. He tucked his head under the blanket as if he were a boy hiding from prowling monsters. Desperately, he hoped he would dream of Shelly when he fell asleep. If he couldn't have her again in the daylight, surely his brain could lie to him while he slept.

But if he dreamed at all, he didn't remember when he woke up. His eyes were thickly crusted, and his face felt swollen. He suspected he'd been crying in his sleep again. Until Shelly left, he hadn't even known that was a thing people did.

Sometime during the night, he'd straightened out his limbs. It was early, the edges of the French doors still dark. He should get up, he supposed, but why? He realized belatedly he'd broken Jaciee's cardinal rule last night and not set up the coffee pot before going to bed. The idea of rinsing out the pot and refilling the coffee now seemed an insurmountable task.

Besides, he couldn't really feel his body. He was conscious he must still be lying there on the mattress, under the sheets, but somehow, he was detached from his own bones. Finding the edges of himself, reattaching his animus to his muscles, and propelling himself out of the bed was an impossibility. He lay in the dark, staring at what might be the ceiling or might be the sky or might be the underbelly of the earth and let pain drink him deep, deep down.

Eventually, he became aware of the sheets resting on his skin, the pull of his neck where his head stretched on the pillow, the weight of the blanket on his upright toes. He swung his legs over the edge of the bed and got up.

Move, said something deep and urgent in his cells, and he did. Light switch. Toilet. Sink. Clothes. He stumbled to the kitchen and swore bitterly at the coffeepot as he rinsed out the pitcher and put a fresh filter and grounds in the basket and pushed the little red button. He leaned against the counter and stared out the back door window as he waited.

Morning grayed. It was funny, he thought, how the world lost its definition in the twilight. It was as if everything blurred. This must be why so many cultures had a mythos around those in-between hours. If even the trees and rocks took on unfamiliar shapes, it wasn't such a leap to imagine graves could loosen their hold on the dead and the gates to the world of fae might swing free, if only for a few moments. He wished, dully, he believed in such things.

It had been nice of Melodie to go with him last night to pick out the flowers. He didn't know whether he'd been that considerate when he was twenty. He'd never been mean—it wasn't in his nature—but he hadn't always paid attention to other people. Even now, he tended to tune folks out and focus on creatures that lived much longer and much shorter lives than most people did—flowers, trees, and calendars measured in blooming and fallowing.

Melodie wasn't like that. She saw other people and what they were feeling, and she listened to what they said and didn't say. It was a good thing there were better people in the world than him. He measured his own virtue more in what he didn't do than what he did. How he didn't produce too much waste or too much carbon or do too much harm.

He was a planter who brought beauty to life, which was a good thing.

Maybe one day, he'd grow into someone like Melodie. Today, he wasn't sure he had enough energy to eat breakfast.

Eventually, he noticed the coffeepot had stopped spluttering. He poured himself a cup and doctored it up like Shelly would have done. He made a face at the first swallow and laughed despite himself, dumping the concoction out in the sink. He'd thought drinking the syrupy mess might make him feel close to her, but it only turned his stomach. He tried again, with a simple black brew, and the familiar bitterness braced him. That was better.

He wandered into the living room on bare feet, opening the

curtains to let the darkness of the house escape into the brightening day. He looked at the recliner and the blanket folded up on the couch beside it. A few weeks ago, he hadn't known how he would survive into the next hour, and now he'd made it out the chair and back into their bed. A little further down this road that probably led nowhere but kept dragging him out of the wilderness, all the same.

He shut his mind against all sense of the calendar. It would be too easy to keep a running tally in his head: How many weeks, how many days, how many hours since Shelly left? He didn't want to know how many of his breaths stood testament to his solitude. If he could, he'd forget the date she died. Let it sink into obscurity, outshone in every way by her life. That might be too ambitious. He wasn't sure. He knew many people made annual memorials of death days, as if the departure needed to be celebrated or grieved fresh. He didn't want that.

Shelly would be no more or less dead in April than in August. He would miss her all the same, regardless of what blossomed or withered. He wouldn't make her death the point of her memory. Yes, this year, somewhere between late summer and early fall, everything had ended for her. But last fall, she bought a purple and green lamb's wool scarf at the farmers' market. Three years ago, they'd gone to the city to see some musical he couldn't remember but she had loved. One year, they'd flown out to California wine country in late September and stayed in bed-and-breakfasts and came home with boxes of Cabernet and Riesling and Chardonnay.

Hayden didn't know how to get through these days, and he wasn't even sure he would, in the end. Sometimes, he was sure his heart squeezed so tight, it had to burst apart. Other times, he thought his lungs might give up on processing air. It took so much effort and energy to stay alive than he thought he had. But if he did muddle on, he wanted to muddle on thinking of the days Shelly had lived, not be consumed by the moment she died.

Whatever she had done, however she had hurt him, Shelly

deserved that. Even the sullen kurinji was remembered for its lush purple flowers, though it only bloomed once in twelve years.

And Shelly had made a garden of his life in so many ways, coloring his days and filling the air he breathed with a sweet fragrance all her own. It turned out he bloodied his hands on this-tles he hadn't seen beneath the petals. He wouldn't trade the years of beauty to save himself the scratches.

Hayden Hill drank his coffee and thought of ashes and water rising like blood through the veins of a strong young oak tree, enriched by the person he had known.

CHAPTER 25

Hayden stopped for a box of bagels and some flavored cream cheeses on the way to the office—more of a way to fill the time than a generous act. He'd gotten up much too early, and the day stretched before him like a desert. He couldn't stand staying in the house any longer, so he drove to the good bakery on the far side of town and took the long way to work.

Jason opened the door for Hayden, whose arms were full; the bagels were balanced on one elbow, and a cloth sack full of salsa jars dangled from the other.

"Should I beware of Greeks bearing gifts?" he asked with a grin.

"Only if you're gluten intolerant or have a fear of spicy food," Hayden said. "I put my vegetable garden to bed this weekend, and I figured most people would rather have salsa than squishy tomatoes or spaghetti sauce."

"You know I always like it hot," Jason said, punctuating his words with a butt wiggle.

"I know nothing of the sort," Hayden laughed. "And I don't want to know. Here, can you put this stuff out in the breakroom and let everyone know it's here?"

"Sure. I'll text the crews. Are you going to be in the field or the office today?"

"We should be wrapping things up at the hospital this week, so I'll probably head over there tomorrow. Today, I'll be working on our seasonal adjustments, and I'll need your help with that."

"You betcha. Just let me know what I can do."

Hayden hadn't thought he was hungry, but the smell of warm yeasty bread had been working on his stomach during the drive over. He was slathering an everything bagel with roasted red pepper cream cheese when a text buzzed from his phone. He deposited his breakfast on his desk and refilled his coffee tumbler from the carafe Jason kept warm before checking the message.

It was from Rachel.

> Thanks for the salsa and chips. It was a good thing Melodie stashed mine for me. The kids already ate all theirs.

A reluctant grin broke over Hayden's face. That was good, at least. He tapped out a quick response:

> No worries. You know how tomatoes are. We could probably solve world hunger with a hundred or so tomato plants. ;o)

> One more reason for me to stick to flowers. Nothing strikes fear in my heart like coming home to a basket of zucchini or tomatoes some coward has dropped off.

> Could be worse. Could be brussels sprouts.

> You're right. That would be worse. They must be harder to grow because that's never happened to me. Yet. Knock on wood.

Hayden sent back a laughing emoji. Before Shelly died, he'd hardly ever used emojis. They were mostly for kids, weren't they?

Influencers or whatever. But now emojis were a kind of communications lifeline. Summoning words that would reassure his family and friends was more than his brain could manage most days. Every time he smiled or laughed, he felt the stretch of every cell of skin across his muscles, heard the jarring sound rattle around his skull like dried seeds in a gourd. With the right emoji, he could almost pull off the appearance of a normal human person. He could almost come across as functional. Too bad there was no emoji function for in-person life. Oh, well. He would take what he could get.

Right now, Hayden had to summon some actual functionality, not just the mirage. With the summer season winding down, it was time to pare down the crew to the year-round staff and review the winter accounts. Lawnmowing services and tree-trimmers often switched over to snow and ice removal to maintain a steady flow of work through the winter, but Hayden's focus was more garden-specific. He enjoyed the slower pace and intimacy of the cold-season schedule. He usually lost a few of the summer employees from one year to the next, as some of them would shift over to more labor-intensive jobs that could provide year-round employment, but others picked up various temporary positions and were eager to return as soon as spring broke through. His core group, though, had been with him for years. Losing one of them always felt like losing a limb. Luckily, it didn't happen often.

The first step would be going through the accounts to see how much winter maintenance would be necessary. Every year, his company added a few more locations, so the size of the permanent crew expanded, too. Even with the tasks required through the colder months, the work wouldn't be considered full-time by any other standards, but he paid full-time wages all the same. He couldn't very well ask people to be available for less than they could live on. And they worked like horses during the summer, so he figured it all balanced out in the end.

By lunchtime, he had a solid idea of how many employees, besides his supervisors Alex and Eric, he would need to keep over the next few months. Next summer, he might need to hire a third supervisor. Or maybe he should actively pull back, stay small deliberately. Maybe growth wasn't its own good. It wasn't as if he were hurting for money. He'd been running a comfortable profit for decades now, and he and Shelly had paid off the mortgage on the house three years before. This had been a goal she insisted on, and they'd always paid down extra—in the beginning, that might have been ten or twenty dollars a month. Eventually, it had all added up. And when everyone else took out home equity loans, Shelly had insisted they keep the house clear. Now, he was grateful for her foresight. It was amazing, the relief of having shelter. All he had to worry about on that score was scraping together the property taxes every year.

Hayden's thoughts drifted to Blooming Bouquets and the kids huddled in the backroom; he recalled last Thursday's meeting. Outside his window, the day had turned gray even as the sun had risen higher in the sky. It looked cold and grim, and for the next five or six months, it would only get colder and grimmer. Even though they didn't get a lot of snow, the incessant damp chill and gusting winds would be miserable to endure on the streets.

Every year, some story ran on the news about this or that person who'd frozen to death on the streets. Hayden was ashamed, but his only real emotional response to those reports had been a distant regret, and a question about why the person hadn't gone to a shelter instead of staying out in the weather. He hadn't spent much time wondering if there was room in the shelter, if the person would be allowed in, or whether they might fear being assaulted in the shelter more than they feared the cold.

Now, the passing of autumn into the next season had his stomach sick. Already, he felt guilty for the cozy warmth of his office—irrational, perhaps, but inescapable. What would happen if there were more than four people who needed shelter at the flower shop? Rachel had said it was first-come, first-served, but what did that look like?

Hayden pushed down the fear as best he could. Surely, the town council would rule in favor of basic human rights.

Hayden's brain ran round and round on the topic, but it always came back to the same place. People, regardless of their names or their birth certificates or the vagaries of their DNA, shouldn't be forced to freeze or starve, shouldn't be humiliated or assaulted, simply because of who they were. How was that a controversial stance to take?

Okay, he had to stop thinking about this for now. If he was going to be able to help at all, he had to stay solvent. Even simply keeping the doors open at Blooming Bouquets might be out of reach if he didn't manage his affairs properly. The loss of Shelly's income was nothing to sneeze at, though he didn't know when he'd look at the actual numbers.

He pushed back from the desk and walked into the front office. "Hey, Jason, can you get the employee files? Sort them into three stacks, the ones we know will stay on all winter, the ones we know have other plans lined up, and the maybes. I want to let everyone know where they stand by the end of the day."

"Gotcha, boss."

Less than two minutes later, Jason laid three neat stacks on manila folders on Hayden's desk, each neatly color-coded with a transparent tab of red, green, or blue.

"Whoa. That was fast."

Jason grinned. "You're kinda predictable."

Hayden resolved to give the man a raise. And Alex and Eric, too. They held this place together when he couldn't even get his clothes on. They were more than workers—they were roots anchoring him deep in the earth when all his stalks withered. Above and beyond dedication deserved recognition and reward.

"You're the best, Jason. Are there any bagels left?"

Jason pulled a guilty mug. "Afraid not. I can run out and grab something for you if you want."

"That would be awesome. I want to work through lunch so I can do this right." Hayden fished out his wallet and passed Jason his credit card. "A turkey sub from that place on the corner and a tub of full-sugar soda. Have 'em put everything they've got on the sub."

"Will do."

"Feel free to grab something for yourself, too."

"Thanks, but I've been dreaming about the Thai curry and boba tea on Harvard Street. I'll bring yours back first before I go out for mine."

"I'll never understand floating gobs of goo in tea."

Jason laughed. "More for me. Be right back."

Hayden had felt real hunger, a rarity these days, but by the time the younger man returned and quietly deposited the food before slipping back out of the room, he'd lost all sense of his stomach. All his energy was focused on the task at hand. He flipped through one file after another, calculating how many more days or weeks of work each of the temporary workers would have, based on their seniority and general performance. It turned out he would need to keep an additional three employees on a full-time basis over the winter.

This was the hardest part of the process. While he made sure everyone he hired fully understood the seasonal nature of the position, taking a person's paycheck away weighed heavily on him. More so this year than it ever had before. Part of this was because of his newfound understanding and empathy for people living lives much nearer to the precipice of disaster than his own, but part of it was simply that he was a walking wound these days. Everything that could hurt, hurt worse than it ever had.

He changed his mind about making the final decisions today. He needed to talk to Alex and Eric first and get their input. Especially after the last couple of months, they knew better whose work was most valuable, whose lives most precarious.

Another idea sprang to mind. He paid his people fair wages for the region, but he didn't know much, if anything, about their personal circumstances. Who had a sick kid or a laid-up spouse, or who was trying to pay off incarceration debts or credit cards? It would be easy to set up a resource room somewhere here in the office, with nonperishable food and secondhand clothes. Maybe school supplies. Hygiene products. He grimaced. If he hadn't already taken Shelly's clothes to the thrift store, he could have brought them here.

Then again, it was probably best he didn't see them hanging up, or worse, being worn by someone he knew.

He should ask Alex what she thought of the idea. Resources could be available through the winter, too, so even the employees on furlough till spring had some kind of safety net.

Hayden didn't trust himself anymore. Did his ideas make any sense, or were they all weird sops to soothe his conscience for sins he couldn't even name? Maybe it would be more helpful to increase the cost-of-living raises next January. That wouldn't help the summer employees, though. And sometimes people needed a boost, a helping hand over the water, when life required more of them than they could possibly supply through no fault of their own.

Hayden was mildly surprised to find the turkey sub reduced to a few soggy bits of lettuce on the wrapper. Even the requisite bag of chips was only greasy crumbs. He hadn't realized he was eating. That was probably good, he thought. He had a hard time finishing his meals these days.

The clock on the wall claimed it was already four o'clock. Hayden gathered up his jacket and shut off the light, closing the office door behind him. Jason looked up with a smile.

"Call Alex and Eric and let them know I need to meet with them in the morning before they hit their worksites. They can have one of the guys fill in for them till they get there—no need to come in early. I need their input before I make the final decisions on the winter schedule."

"Sounds good, boss. See you in the morning."

"Have a good night, Jason."

Once in his truck, Hayden backed up and drove toward Blooming Bouquets, as if he'd planned to go there all day.

CHAPTER 26

Hayden had to hunt for Rachel when he arrived at the shop. He found her cross-legged on the floor, in the corner by the front window. A wide, terra cotta pot ebullient with blooming succulents lay cradled on her knees. Her braided head was bent, her shoulders hunched. He didn't think she'd even heard the door chime, which made no sense, because he found the volume of the thing utterly obnoxious. He slowed his steps, not wanting to barrel up on her.

"Rachel?"

She raised her head, and her cheeks were wet with tears and her eyes blood-red. She made no move to rise. Hayden crouched down in front of her, her sadness landing in his belly like a swallowed stone. He and Rachel were so different, but he recognized the absence shining in her eyes as a reflection of the same absence he felt.

"Shelly?" God, it felt so strange to say her name to this woman. It was like sharing a lung with a stranger. He didn't know if he would ever get used to it, if it would ever hurt any less to know his wife had given a piece of herself to someone else, a piece she'd kept sacrosanct from him.

Rachel nodded bleakly. Hayden dropped lower still. He

couldn't cross his legs like hers, so he maneuvered himself across the aisle and stretched them out. He looked away, focusing on a collection of tiny branching bonsai trees, and waited.

Rachel's voice was low as she spoke. "She insisted on the succulents. That cactus. I'm not a big fan. But Shelly said we needed something for the black thumbs. For people who couldn't possibly keep anything more delicate alive but still wanted a connection to nature. To life."

As uncomfortable as it was to say Shelly's name to this woman, it was more uncomfortable to hear it fall from Rachel's lips. Somehow, it was also reassuring, somehow affirming of Shelly's power of presence in the world. Hayden didn't suppose there was anyone else in the universe who loved Shelly half as much as he did, no one else who missed her as much.

"There's something to that," he said. "She told me my dislike for cut flowers was elitist. She was mostly joking, but it's true that she would have killed even chrysanthemums herself. Maybe she had a soft spot for the black thumbs."

Rachel smiled weepily. "The whole evolutionary development of plants requires absolutely zero input from humans to survive. But somehow, she could still wipe them out."

Hayden's lips twitched despite himself. "It was a special gift. As asteroids to dinosaurs, so was Shelly to plants."

From the corner of his eye, he watched Rachel's fingers toy with a broad, sage-green leaf, fat and smooth with hidden waters. "Tough and seemingly impenetrable, even prickly, but full of secret springs."

Hayden's faint smile vanished. Secret springs. Well of waters sweet or poison, he didn't know anymore. But what he wouldn't give for one more drop on his tongue.

"Yeah." He pushed himself back onto his feet, lifting the pot from Rachel's lap as he stood. He slid it into the empty space on the shelf where its price tag proclaimed its name. He held out his hand, and she took it. Her slender, cool fingers were strong as she pulled herself up. For a weird, irrational moment, he wanted to hang onto her, but he let go.

She wiped her face and sniffed, straightening her shoulders as she faced him. "You didn't come here to talk succulents and cry on the floor. What do you need, Hayden?"

He appreciated the push back into his corner. It felt safer there.

"I've been thinking about this vote with the town council. Which way do you think it will go?"

She shrugged and turned away. "Honestly? I'm not known for happy, hopeful optimism."

"And here I've been calling you Rachel Rainbow in my mind."

She snorted. "Uh-huh. I'd like to think common sense and basic human decency would prevail, especially after so many vulnerable and marginalized people put themselves on the line by speaking up at that hearing, but I anticipate more callousness than compassion from this community."

"Even if that means they'd give up federal funding?"

"That is literally the only scrap of hope I cling to. Maybe simple capitalist greed will prevail, and they'll stick with the money. But there's also a niggling voice in the back of my mind saying if they had less money, that would mean less services, which probably doesn't have a downside as far as they're concerned. People complain the city already makes it too cozy for the homeless here. If they had even fewer beds to offer and more people starved or froze to death on the street, all the better. A quiet culling."

"Damn, woman. You weren't joking about the cynicism."

"Hey, prove me wrong. I'll be happy to celebrate."

"What happens if they pass this resolution and start enforcing these anti-transgender policies?"

"I mean, not much. The city has already been enforcing them —that's why my supply room has beds in it. But now that they've been called out on it, they must embrace it and lose the dollars or reverse course. If they vote it down, then we can get into the shelter as volunteers or observers or board members or whatever and ensure that substantive reform is real. But if they choose to give up the money and hang onto the bigotry, we don't have anywhere to go."

Something like relief tingled in Hayden's veins as he watched the now-familiar anger drown out the grief in Rachel's sparking gaze. He could cope so much better with angry Rachel than with sad Rachel.

"It seems crazy our town services could basically be taken over by a church. Or a collection of churches," Hayden said.

"Small local governments have long provided cover for bigots. Look at the Klan."

"Yikes."

"Exactly." She tipped her head. "Is that the only reason you came? To talk about the shelter?"

He waved vaguely at the window. "It's getting colder out there. I was at work, and I couldn't stop thinking about it. And it's not like I have anywhere else to be."

"I'm about to close up here. Do you—do you want to grab dinner somewhere?"

"God, no." The words tumbled out before he could catch them. "Damn it. I'm sorry. That'd be weird."

Rachel laughed, a real, loud rippling laugh. Hayden thought it was the first time he'd ever heard genuine amusement from her. "No apology needed. I don't even know why I asked. I was terrified you'd say yes as soon as I heard myself offer."

"Hey, we agree on some things. See you Thursday, then?"

"You're coming to the vote?"

"Hell, yes. Couldn't keep me away now."

"All right. See you Thursday."

As Hayden walked out and climbed into the driver's seat of his truck, his own words echoed in his mind. *We agree on some things.* They'd agreed on Shelly. Except Rachel had known all along Shelly wasn't free to build a life with her alone. While he had genuinely believed it was only the two of them against the world.

Under other circumstances, he'd have probably liked Rachel. That bright fury of hers was oddly warming. Shelly, to his chagrin, had been the liar. Rachel was transparent to the point of discomfort. And while her approach was completely different from his own, she was a gardener, too. Someone who listened to the breathing of plants and heard a language they comprehended.

But there were no other circumstances. The only reason their lives had intersected had been Shelly's betrayal. A betrayal Shelly apparently wanted to reveal. Why else would she have written her will the way she did? She couldn't have had any inkling that her death was imminent, but some part of her had wanted to stitch the two disparate parts of her life together.

Rage, now almost as familiar as grief, swelled as he pulled into the driveway at home. Why would she have thought that death would somehow grant her the license to force together two people with warring motives? Two people she'd hurt by using the other? Hayden slammed the truck door shut harder than he intended. It wasn't fair, but no amount of arguing would reverse anything, bring Shelly back, or make her only his.

But no judge heard his case, no scales took measure. Shelly had cheated on him, and she was dead, and he would never hear from her lips any explanation of what she'd been thinking or intending. He'd never have the chance to consider forgiveness, or beg her to stay, or understand why, why, why she'd done this.

Exhaustion burned through him, visceral and crippling. He scraped and scraped at the bottom of the bowl that was his soul, but nothing remained to eat. Still, he couldn't stop, and the grating sound, the raw abrasion, reverberated agonizingly through every cell of his body. He dropped his clothes at the front door and went straight to bed, as if he would find Shelly there in the sheets. He wanted to scream and rail, to call her names and demand answers, but he only curled around her absence and lay there, aching, until emptiness itself expelled him. He paced the floor long into the wee hours of the morning, but his leaden feet could not carry him out of the house of grief.

CHAPTER 27

The week dragged. Time was a saguaro cactus, hoarding hours deep in its belly and eking them out as slowly and painfully as possible. Work got done, at least. That was some sort of consolation, but Hayden hardly cared. Having to pretend the ordinary obligations of life mattered was almost harder than pretending he could breathe without Shelly.

He didn't catch Jason peeking around his office door as often as he had a few weeks ago, and Alex and Eric laughed out loud around him, so he figured he was doing a decent job of fooling everyone. The quickest way to put anyone at ease when they asked how he was doing was to smile and respond, "As well as can be expected."

Invariably, relief lit their eyes, and they rushed hastily to whatever topic had forced them into the company of the bereaved in the first place, a space they'd no doubt have avoided at all costs if they could. He didn't think anyone heard him, not really, or maybe they'd never thought about what those words meant.

As well as can be expected was pretty damn awful. How did people expect him to be when his wife, his best friend, his partner, was a pile of ash under a tree in the backyard?

As well as could be expected. They expected him to push on, stiff upper lip, man up, forge ahead. To do his job, make and spend his money, and not make anyone else uncomfortable by collapsing into a fetid, fly-riddled heap of composting person. Grief, he had learned, robbed him of all his identifiers. He wasn't a man, wasn't a husband, wasn't a friend, wasn't an employer, wasn't a brother. He was nothing but pain: unbearable, inexorable pain.

Even so, the cactus of time did at last surrender its dammed seconds, one at a time. Hayden arrived early at the town council building. Already, the place was milling with people, standing around in the bleak hallways, waiting to be let in. Amazing how this humble little hall, with its stained Berber carpet, dingy white walls, and cheaply framed photos of past mayors would decide who mattered and who didn't, who might die on the streets and who might survive, who could claim an autonomy of being and who couldn't, who had to accept the imposition of others on their own spirits and names.

Hayden recognized many faces, but there were new ones, too. No public statements would be allowed tonight—just the vote— and Hayden was surprised to see so many people. Many of them carried cardboard signs, and Hayden realized both sides had come prepared for protests, based on the outcome. He hadn't considered that possibility.

Like the faintest kiss of a zephyr on the back of his neck, Hayden felt the energy in the hall behind him shift. He turned to see Rachel striding towards him, her hand gripping Mateo's. Her steps didn't slow as she entered the melee, and people parted for her without exception. As usual, even the air around her seemed alive, on fire, alight with electricity. Her chin was up, her shoulders set, and her gaze rock steady. Mateo's face was grim, and his shoulders hunched defensively. He looked incredibly young. Hayden wondered for the thousandth time how the boy's parents could leave him out in the world with no defense or help at all.

Both held signs. Hayden craned his neck to read the upside-down lettering. *Trans Rights are Human Rights* and *Y'all means All.* A slight grin bit into his cheek.

Rachel walked right up to him, raising an eyebrow. "Not prepared, were you?"

"Honestly, it never even occurred to me."

She dropped Mateo's hand and dug into her pocket. "Here." She tossed a set of car keys at him. "I have extras in the back. You can throw what you don't grab into the bed for any other stragglers. Yellow Subaru Baja."

Hayden snort-choked on a laugh. "Of course, it is."

"What?" She glared at him.

He held up his hands. "Nothing, nothing. I'll be right back."

She hadn't been kidding. The woman was nothing if not prepared. Hayden thought there had to be at least ten signs shoved behind the seat of the ridiculous, little truck-ish thing she drove. He grabbed two for good measure—*This Is What A Trans Ally Looks Like*, and *Punks Respect Pronouns*—and tossed the others into the truck bed before heading back in. Heaven knew he was no punk, but maybe someone else in there was.

By the time he returned, the last dregs of the crowd were pushing their way into the hearing room. A handful of open seats remained, but Rachel and Mateo stood against the back wall. Hayden hurried over.

"You don't want to grab a seat?"

Rachel shook her head. "We have more flexibility this way. And it's safer. You never know when a protest might turn ugly."

"You really think people would try something here?"

"You do remember the U.S. Capitol, don't you?"

Hayden grimaced. "Fair point."

Mateo waved at someone across the room. "Sage and Valkyrie are here."

The teenagers squeezed beside Mateo. Their found family felt incomplete without Melodie, who had come down with some kind of stomach bug. Her parents, though, were holding up *Protect Trans Kids* signs on the other side of the room. Hayden thought Sage looked a little drifty—was that a word? And his nose wrinkled at the strong odor of marijuana as they passed him.

He couldn't blame them for wanting to take the edge off before coming in here. Valkyrie looked grim, her jaw set and eyes deliberately cold, her usual anxiety nowhere to be seen

"We got this," Rachel told them fiercely. They all linked hands, leaning the wooden handles of the signs against their legs or the wall behind them. After a brief hesitation, Hayden reached for Rachel's free hand and gripped it firmly. She met his eyes with no surprise at all in her steady gaze, only solidarity.

A sudden sense of surrealism seized Hayden. Three months ago, he'd have never been able to picture himself hanging out with a bunch of trans kids and his wife's lover, fighting for fair treatment and compassion for the homeless. Now, he felt as if this was somehow the one place in the world besides his garden where he still belonged. There was no question he was a transplant in this little plot of earth, a non-native interloper. But noninvasive, he hoped. Maybe in time he'd even become a contributor to healthy biodiversity. A crooked grin ghosted over his lips. Might be the only circumstance in which a white, straight, upper-middle-class man could contribute to diversity.

Rachel squeezed his hand briefly with her cool grip before dropping it. He didn't understand how it was possible for this woman to simultaneously make him feel safe and sick to his stomach, but somehow, she did.

A woman with a face like knots of uncooked dough, with little bits pinched off where the eyes and mouth should be, led the meeting. Hayden remembered her from the last meeting. He still couldn't make out her motivation. She might be disgusted with the inconvenience of the question, or she might be on some sort of moral crusade to annihilate all the perverts, deviants, and pagans. Hayden couldn't tell, and he wasn't sure which was worse. Empathetic apathy or bigot-fed hatred? It was a toss-up.

There were two or three other issues to be voted on first, and naturally, they saved the question of the homeless shelters for last. Hayden tried to convince himself they'd have done so no matter which way they intended to vote; there was little question of the evangelicals and suburban bigots being any less virulent in their dismay than the trans community and their allies. Hayden couldn't deny the sinking feeling in his gut, though, when they finally read the proposition aloud and called for votes.

Seven council members. Six ayes; one resigned, grim-faced nay.

Their little town would rather turn down federal dollars and shutter services for the most desperate members of the community than proffer dignity to people they didn't understand.

Hayden forced himself to look around him at the faces of the people affected. Sage looked murderous. Rachel's whole body hummed with fury, but her eyes were shining. Mateo and Valkyrie openly fought tears. For his own part, Hayden was simply stunned by this inescapable proof of complete disregard for human life. It was downright baffling how this demographic widely regarded a barely formed fetus as easier to love than the person standing right in front of them.

On the other hand, maybe it wasn't baffling at all. The baby required nothing of them besides control of the mother, and control over mother's bodies—or the bodies of potential mothers —this was the gold standard in their ideology. A trans person in need of food, shelter, or kindness required them to dig into their pockets and into their hearts. Apparently, that was too much to ask.

Obviously, the universe would crumble, God would be crippled, God's followers would become persecuted victims of unspeakable horrors, if any of them were asked to address someone by a particular prefix or offer them a safe bed to sleep in.

Hayden pulled himself up. He was going dark, spiraling down a tunnel as hate filled as the one these vermin had crawled from. This wasn't about them. In his own mind, at least, he refused to let this question be defined by the ignorance and vitriol of people he didn't even know.

He was here for Mateo, for Sage and Valkyrie, for Rachel, for every person who needed a little help to get by and asked to be treated with common human dignity in the process. He wasn't here to fight hatred. He was here to stand for love.

His gaze slid sideways. Rachel probably wasn't feeling the same. That was her prerogative, for sure. He imagined fury and rage could provide a fine propellant when despair threatened to mire the wheels into immobility. But he was too damn tired to summon anger as a motivator. Even his anger at Rachel, his loathing and envy, faded and swelled unpredictably along with the wholly unwelcome sensations of liking and camaraderie.

As protestations swelled, the sound of a gavel pounding on the table swallowed up the shouts.

"Sit down," Rachel yelled, yanking at his shoulder as she raised her sign over her head and dropped into a cross-legged position on the floor.

Hayden didn't understand, but he followed suit. It hadn't occurred to him both sides would erupt into fury no matter what the outcome, but that seemed to be exactly what was happening. Even though the anti-trans lobby had won the day, they were apparently incensed that anyone supporting equal rights for trans people still existed, and certainly that they would dare to voice any displeasure over the decision. Freedom of speech and assembly and the whole troublesome Constitution only existed when it could be used as a brick through the window or a lash on the spine.

Hayden quickly realized the pro-equal-rights protestors were on the floor, while the victors in tonight's vote were surging angrily toward the exit. One clear route through the hall to the doors in the rear of the auditorium had been left open, but the crowd stalled. Hayden saw swinging handbags and raining fists, while the people on the floor raised their signs protectively over their heads and chanted in unison, governed by some emcee he hadn't observed.

"Trans rights are human rights! Trans rights are human rights!"

He leaned close to Rachel and yelled, "Wouldn't it be safer if we stood up? These people are going to run over us."

She shook her head. "The cops will be looking for a reason to haul us in. Sitting down forces the assholes to be the aggressors. We'll always be first in cuffs unless we take precautions. And maybe even then."

Sure enough, as if summoned by her words, what appeared to be the town's entire tiny police force rushed into the room with a syncopa of unintelligible, guttural yells. Hayden peered from under his sign but couldn't tell what was happening besides the additional bodies joining the melee. He noticed the council table was empty; the officials had snuck out the back door.

Eventually, the space emptied of the victors, none in handcuffs, although the officers must have seen clear instances of assault. Once all the church deacons, neighborhood-watch members, and PTA moms were ushered out, the police yelled at the rest of them to stand up and exit the building. Hayden had the distinct impression they weren't treated differently because they'd behaved differently, but simply to limit potential chaos. If anything, the cops seemed as fed up with their group as with the people who'd been attacking them.

"They can kick us out of the building, but not off the sidewalk. And we have better visibility out here, anyway," Rachel shouted urgently in Hayden's direction as they all piled out the hallway and into the night. The autumn air was cool and crisp, but Hayden welcomed the rush of air. Sweat ran freely between his shoulder blades, and his legs shook. He hadn't realized how stressed he was.

He couldn't imagine what this felt like for Sage and Valkyrie and Mateo. It was one thing to protest for equal rights as someone whose access had never been in question. Hayden figured the absolute worst-case scenario was some pepper spray in the face, or getting booked into jail for a short time. Trans kids lived with the daily reality of possible violence. What did it do to a person's psyche, to live with that continual knowledge and fear, to have to stay alert and take precautions just to go to the store, get the mail, or apply for a job? And God forbid they try to enjoy themselves and head out to a club or hike a wilderness trail or go to a concert. Online dating with its predators and fetishists had to be a whole other nightmare.

Hayden didn't recognize the pieces of himself that insisted he show up tonight. He'd never protested anything before. He didn't consider himself a political person, didn't pay much attention to the news. Tonight, though, everything felt different.

Something wild and alight bubbled along his veins. Suddenly, there was no way he could remain still and silent while people in his own community, his own town, went cold or hungry or faced physical threats and existential despair when his presence might help.

Somebody had brought a megaphone and now led their little crowd in chants as they marched up and down the sidewalk in front of the building. The moneyed pigs, as Hayden spontaneously decided to think of them, waddled their chunky little asses to their nice cars and drove home to their brick houses, where they would no doubt guzzle wine while they looked out their windows and watched gleefully as the big bad wolf gobbled everyone they'd locked out. That old story took on a completely different construction than Hayden had ever considered before. Maybe it was less about the difference between sloth and hard work, and more about access to resources and general lack of compassion.

Hayden ended up kind of disappointed in his first protest. The few reporters present snapped photos, grabbed a couple of click-bait quotes, and took off to tweet their stories. This part of town was quiet outside of business hours; in fact, the whole town was quiet after eight p.m. Southern small towns weren't exactly notorious for their night scenes. The group grew smaller, and eventually, the person with the megaphone promised to post any updates about future protests or next steps on their Facebook page.

He walked Rachel and the three kids—he supposed he should stop calling them that, but they seemed so young—back to her car.

Mateo, at least, really was a kid, only fifteen years old. It still boggled Hayden's mind that his parents let him go. Hayden offered to give them a ride back to the shop so Rachel could go straight home, but Rachel said she didn't mind the extra driving. They were more comfortable with her than with him, anyway. They probably wanted to download and debrief after the emotionally draining night. Hayden drove home alone.

The house was completely dark when he pulled into the drive. Streetlights and starlight streamed gently across the rocky xeriscape, picking out sparkling hues in the various facets of the stones. He parked the truck and eschewed the garage door, going through the back gate into the backyard.

The world was closing in on itself, pulling all its color and moisture deep into its belly in preparation for the coming winter. Hayden couldn't see that now, but he could hear it in the quiet inhalations and exhalations of brittle leaves and drying stalks and the whispering sheaves of decorative grasses. What looked like death was only a refusal to surrender. Adaptation, metamorphosis. Transfiguration.

Bleakly, he wondered if he would recognize Shelly when he met her again. In the silvery dust drifting from a moth's wing, in the first acorn of the young oak, in rainbow glints bubbling on foaming surf. If what remained of her would perceive anything familiar in him.

He sounded like some mad reincarnationist. All cells were recycled in the end, and all that was real was somehow preserved. Right? That wasn't philosophy; that was fundamental science.

Hayden didn't know what a particle of love looked like, but it tasted like sand. Rolling around in his mouth, the grit burrowing deep into folds of tissue, impossible to swallow, impossible to spit out. A continual discomfort, a comforting continuity.

CHAPTER 28

Almost two weeks passed before Hayden saw Rachel again. He had many people to meet in the meantime: lawyers and accountants and account managers. He wanted his thoughts clear and organized before he talked to her, and Rachel Lundgren had a way of muddying his processes. She was like a snapdragon: ebullient, brash, persistent. And like an actual dragon, prone to sudden fits of scorching and making a great mess wherever she found herself, with her massive, leathery wings and clawed feet.

Hayden didn't know if he'd ever be comfortable with either her presence or her existence. Mostly, he hated her—or at least, the concept of her. He loathed her with wretched, sick envy that turned his stomach and seethed through his veins. He couldn't see her, couldn't think of her without imagining her and Shelly together. Without wondering for the thousandth time about all the small betrayals Shelly had inflicted, the lies she'd told, the secrets she'd given away to this stranger. He wanted to know what in him Shelly had despised, what she had resented, so he could despise and resent it, too.

Other times, though, Rachel steadied him. That mad energy of hers functioning like a gyroscope. He saw things with her he hadn't seen before. And as much as he wished it weren't true, she was a thread tying him to his dead wife he was reluctant to snip.

He had no idea how Rachel felt about him. He hadn't thought about it. It was all he could do these days to keep his own feelings from drowning him. She probably humored him in the hopes of keeping his investment secure in Blooming Bouquets.

He didn't really believe that, though. She'd let him in much further than she'd needed to. In some ways, maybe her burden was greater than his. The time she'd had with Shelly was much shorter than his had been.

Good, he thought bitterly. He hoped she was suffering more than him. He didn't know how that was possible, but he could dream. If nothing else, he wanted her to hurt at least as bad as he did.

Whatever was possessing him to concoct this scheme to entangle his life more with hers—well, he'd be hard-pressed to explain it.

He did try, with Lorne and Jaciee. They came over for pizza, beer, and bad movies on Friday night. Jaciee had Snapple, and Hayden had laughed when he saw her carrying a case of the glass bottles into the house.

"I don't think I've drunk that stuff since we were in college."

She shrugged. "Cravings. I'm leaving these over here. Keep some cold for me, all right? When I need 'em, I need 'em."

"Small price to pay for being an uncle. I think I can find some room in the fridge."

Jaciee snorted. Since Hayden had finally cleaned out the various plasticware and tins from well-meaning friends and colleagues, his refrigerator was painfully bare, and Jaciee knew it.

Hayden waited till the teenagers on the television screen were panting and blood-splattered in the woods before broaching the subject.

"I'm going to build a homeless shelter."

"What?"

Jaciee shot straight up on the couch beside him. Lorne was a beat behind, his gaze still transfixed on the screen as he munched on a folded-up slice of pizza. His wife's reaction prompted him to look around confusedly.

"What?" he echoed.

"I'm going to build a homeless shelter. Or, at least, help build one."

"That's ambitious, and kind of random," Jaciee said.

"Not as random as it seems." Hayden's words rambled a bit like blackberry bushes, but he managed to explain in there-and-back-again fashion about the impromptu shelter at Blooming Bouquets, what Mateo was enduring, what Shelly had been trying to do. What he now wanted to do, too. As incomprehensible as it was, Rachel was an integral part of who he was becoming.

Lorne paused the movie, and he and Jaciee listened intently, interrupting often with questions. To Hayden's surprise, they seemed to be trying to understand, not to dissuade. Wryly, Hayden wondered if his little brother hadn't been miles ahead of him all along.

"Beds and a kitchen are a start. Sort of," Hayden rattled off ideas. "They're the essentials of not dying. But if we want people to live fully, we need more. A room with a wide variety of clothing suitable for work of different types. Computers to enable people to apply for jobs or do schoolwork. Mailboxes so they can list the shelter as a mailing address. Twenty-four-hour nursing and counseling staff for triage. I'm thinking a nurse-practitioner and a psychiatrist, so people don't find themselves lapsing on their meds. We could have weekly support groups run by the residents themselves, for addictions or trauma survival or whatever they need."

"Wow." Jaciee slapped Lorne's hand away from the last slice of pizza and snagged it for herself. "That sounds expensive. And complicated."

"It will be."

"What's the plan?" Lorne asked. "How can we help?"

Hayden looked down. Damn, he easily cried these days. He swallowed and went on.

"There's gonna be a ton of paperwork and bureaucracy groveling to start with. Lots of meetings with people who know way more about this than me. Emails to send."

Jaciee squeezed Hayden's knee. "Just say the word. We'll show up and do what we can. Organization isn't exactly your strong suit. Maybe I can help with some of that."

Hayden grinned abashedly. "I can't argue with you there."

"What about the money, though?" Lorne asked his wife's question again.

"Well, Shelly had a substantial life insurance policy, and she had a lot of other investments as well. You know we own the house, so I don't have to worry about payments there. We'll still have to get donations and maybe grants, but I can at least begin the work."

"This sounds like a full-time job. Can you really swing this and keep your business running?"

"I probably can't do either, honestly. I've been trying to decide whether to expand the business, and the answer is yes. I need to hire someone to help manage the extra business. And as far as the shelter goes, I'm the last person who needs to oversee that. Hopefully, I can find the right people and lend my support. And help drum up the money, obviously."

Jaciee nodded slowly. She had already adopted a habit of rubbing her tummy, though Hayden still couldn't make out any sign of the little life unfurling in there.

"That makes sense," she concurred. "I'm sure there are loads of qualified, passionate people who simply lack the resources. You could be a kind of silent partner, apart from fundraising."

"Staff gardener."

Lorne raised his eyebrows. "Oh, there has to be a garden, too?"

"Of course. Everybody needs a little dirt under their nails. We could grow our own fresh vegetables and herbs and sell the surplus at the farmers' market. Make a little money and get some positive self-promotion at the same time."

Lorne chuckled. "Sounds like you've been thinking about this an awful lot."

"Obsessing, probably."

Jaciee and Lorne shared a look. Hayden knew they'd been worried about him since Shelly died. He couldn't tell if this new passion reassured them or further perturbed them.

"I guess we'll meet this Rachel person at some point, if she's going to be your new partner." Lorne raised an eyebrow. "I mean, she's already your partner with the flower shop, but this is a whole other level of involvement."

"Ah, yeah."

Jaciee poked him. "What does that mean?"

"I haven't exactly talked to her about it yet."

"That seems like a pretty big oversight."

"I wanted to have everything in order before I broached the idea. I mean, not everything, but something. I talked to my money people, at least, and a couple of attorneys and some people at town hall. I want to be able to tell her what's possible before I asked if she wants in."

"That's reasonable. Are you sure you want to work with her?" Jaciee gave him a probing look. "I wouldn't, if I were you."

Hayden shrugged. "I don't, but I can't imagine doing it without her, either. I can't explain it. She's a connection, somehow. Something or someone important, even if it makes me uncomfortable. Besides, she has enough energy for twelve of me. You'll see when you meet her. If she agrees, she'll be a powerhouse for the project."

Lorne gave him a crooked smile. "Kinda sounds like the premise of a Dateline special."

Hayden laughed. "I make no promises. Murder is still a possibility I can't rule out."

"It's not an adventure without a little danger, right?" Jaciee chimed in.

"On that note—" Lorne nodded toward the gape-jawed teenagers frozen on the television screen.

"Why not? A little terror is good for the soul."

"Exactly. Run toward what scares you."

Lorne hit the remote, and they spent the rest of the evening in happy communion with popcorn, viscera, beer, and Snapple. Jaciee fell asleep before the monster could make his final appearance and didn't stir as Lorne and Hayden winced and howled and cackled by turns. It was the first time in weeks Hayden had laughed without the sound choking in his throat like ash.

CHAPTER 29

Much as he dreaded the rapidly approaching winter, Hayden took a strange solace in the dark and foggy mornings of late autumn. He stepped out on the back patio in his bare feet. Cold damp from the concrete seeped into his bones, grounding and reassuring him that he existed in this time and this place. Pain of any sort besides the constant ache in his heart was always a relief. A distraction, however minor.

It would be another hour before the sun was fully up. The stars were faded almost completely, the sky still midnight blue save for the faintest gilding low on the horizon. But the birds had no doubt the day was coming. They sang lustily, and Hayden could hear their little feet and rustling feathers as they hopped from branch to branch and probed the frosty earth for unlucky earthworms.

Almost all the leaves of crimson and russet and orange had fallen and were heaped on the bare ground in glittering piles delineated from the dark by shimmering crystals of frozen dew. The bare branches, outlined by the weak gaze of the streetlamps, held a fierce beauty of their own. By spring, he would be glad to see them dressed again in green, but today, Hayden could commune with their starkness. Stripped of all their costume and comfort, they remained themselves. The beech was still the beech, the willow still the willow, however the seasons stole from them all they had worked so hard to grow and nurture. He, too, was still himself, whatever life had ripped away from him. The greening season would return, even if it felt impossible in the face of all the cold and dark.

He'd followed Jaciee's rule before bed and readied the coffeepot, but it turned out to be unnecessary. Rachel had texted him back this morning, saying she could meet him for coffee before the shop opened. He'd sent an email to Jason to let him know he'd make it to the office late.

Hayden didn't know what he'd do if Rachel didn't want to be a part of the shelter. He'd have to go forward somehow, but as irrational as it might be, he couldn't conceive of the project without her. He thought he could be an icebreaker if he had to, but she was the engine powering the ship through the icebergs. He suspected everyone lucky or unlucky enough to have Rachel Lundgren in their life felt the same way. She was as much a force as a person, and despite all her fury and sharp edges, she invigorated more than she eviscerated.

He shivered as the morning breeze blew through his thin pajama pants. The stars had vanished, and the few leaves still clinging to brittle branches chimed like tiny glass bells. His stomach was uncharacteristically tight. One way or another, he was on the cusp of a massive shift in his life, and he had no idea what to expect.

Naturally, he wound up at the coffee shop early. The wide-mouthed coffee cups looked more like soup bowls than mugs. Didn't they realize that would make the brew cool too quickly? Maybe their other customers didn't like their drinks quite as scalding hot as he did. He ordered a praline roll and picked at it with a fork until he saw Rachel walk in the door. He half-stood and waved. She smiled and tucked her chin toward the counter, indicating she'd get her breakfast before coming to the table.

She didn't look nervous at all, Hayden reflected. And why

should she? Her step was lighter than usual. Hayden hoped this boded well for his massive request.

A few minutes later, she was sitting down with a matching soup bowl, though hers was decidedly lighter in color and dressed with a foam heart. She'd opted for a praline roll, too.

"Great minds," she said.

Hey. An opening. Hayden leapt right in, abandoning his carefully prepared lead-in.

"I hope so. I have a proposal for you."

Rachel eyed him with surprise over the rim of her cup.

"Let me explain first, and you can tell me what you think."

Hayden wished he could stop his brain from trying to interpret Rachel's swiftly changing expressions as he talked. He didn't know why this woman made him so nervous, or why he wanted the nerve-wracking creature as a partner. But she did, and he did. He rattled on, his words coming faster and faster as her eyes narrowed, and her lips pursed, and her head tilted. She ate steadily as he talked, deliberately chewing each tiny bite. Knowing her as he'd come to, Hayden suspected it was a conscious effort to keep from interrupting with questions. If her mouth was full, she couldn't talk. If he hadn't been so anxious, he'd have laughed.

Finally, he stumbled to a full stop, taking refuge in a massive gulp of cooled coffee and trying not to bug his eyes at her in a practical panic.

She took her time, wiping her mouth with her napkin before responding.

"I absolutely want to be part of this."

Hayden exhaled.

"I also have no idea what to do. I researched for months— years really—before I opened Blooming Bouquets. This sounds like a much bigger undertaking."

Hayden nodded. "I feel the same. But I think if we reach out to queer organizations here in town and talk to successful shelters or transitional homes in other areas, we'll find people who know what they're doing. And we can learn as we go."

Rachel tipped her head in assent. "Something like this might take years to get off the ground."

"Almost certainly. But the sooner we start, the sooner we can open. We can't just wait around for someone else to fix the problem. I mean, I'm sorry. I know you've been doing what you can. But me, I can't wait. I have an idea, and a little bit of means. I've got to try. And I think you'd be an enormous asset."

Rachel's mouth widened slightly into a grin. "Thanks."

"We should establish a nonprofit. I'd like to name it after Shelly, but I haven't thought of anything beyond that."

Eyes downcast, Rachel fiddled with her napkin for a few minutes. "What about the Shelly Hill Center for Hope? What you're describing will be much more than a homeless shelter if we can pull this off. It'll be a way out. A way up."

Those stupid tears pricked at him again. God, he hated hearing his wife's name used like a legacy instead of a call she would answer. "I think that's perfect."

Rachel looked at him, then, and Hayden saw he wasn't the only one struggling. Shared grief with a rival had to be the hardest thing he'd ever had to reconcile. In a weird way, as much as it tore him up, it was empowering. He didn't understand it, but he was learning to accept it. Strange gifts from strange gods.

"What do you need from me right now?" Rachel asked.

"Contacts are the main thing. Anyone you know who's already involved in the community, anyone you think might want to help in even the smallest way. My sister-in-law Jaciee is going to help organize, and if I can get my shit together before she gives birth in a few months, I think I can con her into helping me fundraise, too."

Rachel snorted. "Good luck with that. I'm glad it's more than the two of us starting out. There's a reason Shelly was my business partner and not just an investor. Books and files are not my strong point."

"Same," Hayden said. "Luckily, Jaciee is a beast at whatever she attempts—as long as it's not in the kitchen. With her on our side, we're already ahead of the game."

"Cool. What about your brother?"

"Lorne? He's completely on board, but I don't know how useful he'll be outside of moral support. He's a high school teacher, so his plate is perennially full."

"All right. Well, I'll work on a list of contacts."

"In the short-term, the housing situation is only going to get more dire. Probably some people who'd been willing to risk staying in the shelter before will feel more unwelcome and vulnerable now."

Rachel nodded soberly.

"You know," he continued, "I've always had reservations about the safety issues as far as Blooming Bouquets is concerned. And even if you're able to continue without problems, the space is extremely limited. We're a small town, but that's still a problem, especially with winter coming on."

"You could set up bunk beds in one of your spare rooms." Rachel met his gaze.

Hayden was thrown completely off his train of thought. "Are you crazy?" The words popped out before he could stop them.

Rachel laughed dryly. "Just saying. I don't imagine you're lacking for room these days."

"If I was worried about safety issues in your shop, with a locked door between the supply room and the rest of the store, what in the world makes you think I'd be okay with strangers milling in and out of my house?"

"Hey, I'm just spit-ballin' here, looking for solutions. Gotta think outside the box, you know."

Irritation bit at him even as the idea took root. What about Mateo, after all? Hayden liked the young man. And he didn't seem to have drug issues Hayden wasn't equipped to deal with. If anyone needed a safe place to sleep, it had to be a sixteen-year-old whose own family had abandoned him. But then an uglier thought intruded.

"How would it look if an established adult man was taking at-risk teenagers into his house?"

"Let's say you could only house adults. Twenty-one and over."

"You're killing me."

"Not yet," Rachel said sweetly. "Give me time."

"I'm regretting this already."

She grinned, undaunted. She looked fierce – and beautiful, Hayden thought, with her fearless eyes and her freckled cheeks. This must have been how Shelly saw her.

"Maybe—" He paused. "Maybe part of the foundation could assist in transitional housing while we're still working toward the shelter. A certain percentage of our funding could be set aside for hotel rooms on nights when the temperature drops. It wouldn't be much, but it would be something."

"That's actually a good idea. See? You needed me to get the gears working."

"Yeah, yeah."

They said goodbye on the sidewalk outside the café. Rachel was off to the flower shop, and Hayden was going into the office. It was more important than ever to keep his business afloat. It might turn out to be a life raft for more people than just himself and his employees. He had to work on full inflation.

When they parted, they almost hugged, but their bodies arrested at the same moment and simultaneously aborted. Something painfully like friendship vibrated in the empty air between them.

"Later!" Rachel said brightly, fairly tripping over her feet as she backed up.

"I'll be in touch," Hayden promised, hurrying away in the opposite direction.

Strange, strange gods, he thought.

CHAPTER 30

our years later

F Hayden looked into the mirror. Strange to think, the last time he'd worn this suit was at Shelly's funeral. It felt as awkward and ill-fitting as it had then, although the waist and inseam were technically correct. He'd gotten a new tie for the occasion, a rainbow monstrosity Jaciee had picked out. He only had to wear it once; naturally, this once would include TV cameras, but a fashion plate he was not. As soon as this was over, he'd be back in blue jeans and a pullover.

Rachel shifted beside him, a faint sweet fragrance drifting toward him like a gust of anxiety. Hayden grinned to himself. It had been an unexpected and welcome delight to realize that for all her bluster and rage, Rachel was even more uncomfortable on stage than he was. Hayden would take his gifts where he found them.

Lorne and Jaciee and Hayden's little niece, Lisbet, stood at the front of the small crowd that had gathered. Well, Lorne and Jaciee stood. Hayden was quite sure Lisbet had pogo-sticks for legs. She was never still. Behind him, the squat, expansive brick building whose ironwork sign proudly proclaimed *Shelly Hill Center For*

Hope stood on a sweeping green hill. They'd had to settle for a location a little further from town center than they had wanted. Hayden had underestimated both the power and stamina of the "not in my backyard" crowd. Even many of the people who supported the shelter in theory didn't want it visible from their picket fence. The unintended benefit of this was being able to afford a bigger plot, which Hayden ensured meant a bigger garden.

He was determined to have the best and most bountiful vegetables and herbs at the farmers' market. If he couldn't win over folks with words, he'd win with carrots and peppers. How could they call someone deviant who grew the most beautiful squash in town?

He was pleased to see the little column of protestors marching up and down the opposite sidewalk with their cardboard signs. Let 'em shout their ignorance and hate to the world. He liked the contrast.

He poked Rachel. "You ready for this?"

She glared at him. He was impressed that she managed to keep a fake smile pinned to her cheeks even while her eyes drove daggers into him.

"I can't wait for this to be over," she said through clenched teeth, "and you know it."

"I do feel the same, but I can't help enjoying your misery."

"I'm well aware."

Happily, neither of them had to lead the little press conference, as it was. Theirs was the first shelter and transitional center of its kind in the state, so a couple of news channels and capitol newspaper reporters had shown up, in addition to the town rag. One of the first people Hayden had hired once the Shelly Hill Foundation got off the ground was a media manager. Shasta Sullivan was barely more than a volunteer, based on the pittance the foundation paid them, but they worked harder than any CEO. Shasta would be doing most of the talking. Hayden and Rachel were window-dressing, available to answer questions if necessary.

Hayden did have one brief statement to make after Shasta introduced the project and announced the opening.

Hayden looked out over the faces and let his mind wander as the media manager's well-rehearsed words flowed over him. Some in the crowd were allies he'd never realized existed behind the everyday smiles and shallow engagements of ordinary life, folks who emerged from checkout counters and church pews and office buildings to lend a hand and a dollar to help people they didn't know. Some were people who'd been staunch members of the gay community since long before he understood there was such a thing. Alex and Jason were both here, beaming up at him. Near the back he caught sight of Valkyrie, looking restless and fierce at the same time. They'd lost Sage ten months ago to a drug overdose they all tried hard to believe was accidental. It seemed cruel that they'd been so close to offering more help when they lost them. That was the nature of this business, though—every day lost might be a person lost. No one could afford to wait.

Mateo was in his second year at the local community college. He was in classes today, but he'd be here tonight—as staff, not a resident. Hayden's heart swelled with unmerited pride. That kid —that young man, he corrected himself silently—was going to do great things. He had no idea how Mateo managed to do everything he did. And Mateo's mom had even started coming around. Hayden hoped his dad would follow suit, but he didn't know if that would ever happen, or if it should. Maybe the man would only do more harm than good. Hayden wanted to believe love would win out in the end, but that might be naivete on his part.

Melodie lived out west now, in the land of earthquakes, oceans, and deserts. Hayden missed her, but she kept in touch with texts and occasional postcards from the kitschy tourist attractions she visited. She sent a flurry of celebratory gifs to Rachel this morning. Hayden had wanted to tell Rachel about the bouquet of cut flowers from Melodie at his house, but he hadn't been able to get the words out without choking up.

Shasta waved him forward. Rachel shot him a snarky look from under her lashes.

He stepped up to the microphone and cleared his throat. Damn. He sounded like a phlegmy old man. He thanked everyone for being there, and he thanked Shasta for the welcome. "Shelly Hill was my wife and my best friend. And she was a mystery I never unraveled, a flower still blooming when a storm cut her down. In a convoluted way I won't try to untangle for you, she's the one who built this place, even though the first dollar wasn't raised until months after she died. I hope every person who steps through these doors will know she's rooting for them. And I hope everyone who leaves and goes back into the world will carry with them the seeds of her hope and help them to bloom wherever life takes them."

Hayden stepped back beside Rachel amidst a smattering of applause.

"You did good," she whispered, her cheeks wet.

"It's not too late for you to speak if you change your mind," Hayden teased in a voice rough with his own unshed tears.

"Not gonna happen," she hissed back.

With a flourish, Shasta cut the broad pink and blue ribbon stretched across the entrance to the center and flung the doors wide. "Please come in and look around. We'll be happy to show you around and answer any questions you have."

Rachel squeezed Hayden's hand quickly before drawing a deep breath and squaring her shoulders as she led the way in.

Some of the crowd dispersed, but most wandered inside in curious clutches. Hayden, Rachel, and Shasta each took a small group and headed in different directions to point out the various facilities and explain the resources available. Something Hayden hadn't thought of back when they started planning was the satellite offices for several statewide organizations who would send representatives here one or two days a week to provide outreach for their own goals. Especially in such a conservative state, it wasn't always easy to access what was offered, more so when transportation was an issue. Lorne had been pivotal in pulling it together. As a teacher, he understood how many different agencies might be involved in a single person's care, agencies that might not typically interact with each other at all. He and Jaciee had spent countless hours on the phone and in person, persuading organizations and agencies of the urgency of the need.

As Hayden led his group through the halls and rooms, his gaze lingered on the many vases full of colorful, cut blooms. The foundation hadn't paid for those, but he and Rachel had.

The brevity of cut flowers still made him sad, the way their fragrance was stronger and sweeter for the coalescence with death. Shelly had known this as well as he did, but she loved them anyway. Hayden wanted to learn to love what was leaving. He wasn't there yet, but he was trying. He preferred to love in denial of any possibility of an imminent end. Before Shelly died, he hadn't realized that was what he was doing, but now that he knew, it wasn't any easier to let go of the feeling.

The whole affair wrapped up much more quickly than he expected. Rather abruptly, in fact. Before he knew it, he and Rachel were in the empty parking lot, looking at each other with equal expressions of anticlimax.

"Well."

"Doors are open."

"We did it."

"We did. Now we must keep doing it."

Hayden's turn to glare. "Come on. We deserve one afternoon to catch our breath, at least."

"We do. We will. Trivia tonight?"

"Obviously."

Rachel waved and slid into her car. Hayden swung up into his pickup truck cab, but he didn't start the engine as he watched her drive away. Who would have ever thought the best friend he'd wanted to grow old with would have introduced him to his new best friend by breaking his heart in all the worst ways?

He still wasn't sure how it had happened. He and Rachel

Lundgren were like two spiky little cactuses sharing the same bare patch of ground. They'd had to grow up into each other's hard, prickly arms to survive, whether they liked it or not. Mostly, they hadn't liked it. But by depending on each other, they learned to like each other. And then to love each other.

All grief was the same in some ways. Hayden didn't think his heart would ever stop aching when he thought of Shelly. And he thought of her every day. Some days, he thought of her every hour. And her betrayal was a wound that would never heal, either.

He tried not to give in to the thoughts anymore, but more than anything, he wanted her to be here to make sense of it, to explain. To tell him how the hell she could have done that to him. To say she was sorry. To say she was wrong. To make it right. As if that were a thing that could happen.

But there was no sense to be had. No mending. No healing. Every day, he bound up the gaping hole as best he could and worked through the throbbing, burning pain.

Rachel was part of this, and she wasn't. She had turned out to be much more than the catalyst of his agony. As he knew, fairly or not, he was the catalyst of hers. In some truly crazy way, their shared hurts caused by each other's existence became part of the strength they lent each other. Who better than Rachel to understood what he was going through after Shelly died? Who understood Rachel's grief better than he did?

And now, for over a year, they've been going to a weekly trivia night together down at a local bar. Beer and cheese fries could make friends out of almost anyone, Hayden figured.

One of these days, Rachel would start dating seriously again, and that would be weird. How could he explain that he'd feel jealous on Shelly's behalf? That had to be the most convoluted emotional reaction ever. Luckily, he hadn't had to confront it yet. Rachel was still in the same phase he was—infrequent, brief and pointless physical encounters purely to feel less alone for a while.

Lorne and Jaciee had made half-hearted attempts to convince

him to re-enter the dating world, but they'd dropped their attempts eventually. Hayden could think of few possibilities more horrifying than sitting in a café or a bar, looking into eyes that weren't Shelly's, listening to someone else's voice, feeling someone else's hand under his. Meeting someone? Hayden wasn't sure he'd ever meet someone else, ever again. Not really. Not actually intersect with another person and then divert his own path to join up with theirs. That level of intimacy and vulnerability wasn't something he thought he could bear anymore.

Some of the most beautiful trees in the world were sterile, after all. And he had other gardens to till.

CHAPTER 31

S helly's oak tree was new with spring leaves. Hayden sat on the composite bench he'd placed under what would one day be the shade of its spreading branches. Now, just the tips of the many-lobed leaves fluttered in the blue skies overhead. It was only May, but already the air was warm and humid and abuzz with birds and insects.

A couple slices of bread and butter sat on a napkin on his lap —a half-hearted attempt at supper. He'd never gotten back in the habit of actual meals, with no one to share them with. He ate what struck him as tasty when he felt hungry, and that was the extent of it. Some nights when he stopped by the Center, he had supper with the residents, but even then, he usually drank some coffee and maybe munched a cookie and chatted while they ate.

There'd been doubts about the size of the Center back when they'd been in the planning phase, but they were full almost every night. Something they hadn't realized was how many people from surrounding communities would trek in to take advantage of the resources they offered. That was a point of contention with some folks in town, but Hayden didn't pay much attention.

There was no quick fix to trauma, no fast track out of addiction or unhealthy coping mechanisms, but Hayden felt confident they were already beginning to see progress. It had only been a few months, so it was too early to pull numbers. All the same, Hayden knew of several residents who had been steadily working full or part-time jobs for weeks now. Every day, he went in, he saw someone finding clean, gender-affirming clothes that fit. The support groups and counseling sessions were always fully booked. And he often saw the college and trade school reps engaged in intense conversations with hopeful students.

There'd been trouble, too, of course. That was unavoidable wherever people found themselves. One of the first community relationships they'd tried hard to foster had been with the local law enforcement, so when the cops did get called out, they came as partners, not as enemies. This was still a work in progress, but at least it was still a work.

Hayden did believe the numbers would be on their side in the end, but part of him didn't care. If a year from now, they'd succeeded in helping just ten percent of their residents, either by moving off the streets, kicking bad habits, enrolling in school, or just staying alive one more night, he'd considered that a swimming success. Who wouldn't give everything for that ten percent? If you saw ten kids drowning and knew you could only save one if you dove in, how could anyone stay on dry ground?

Unbidden, the image of a ghost orchid rose in his mind.

"I was wrong," he murmured slowly.

The tree limbs fluttered gently in the wind, as if listening to his words. Hayden imagined he could feel the oak breathing in his own chest, in his own lungs.

God. He missed her so much. So much. His skin was raw with the wanting.

"Your beauty was never hidden. Never a secret. You didn't bloom in the dark."

His veins had been the blind little runners, burrowed deep into the safety of black loam and leaf litter. She'd been out there in the sun all along. Wild, reckless bougainvillea.

"I'm gonna try to stay in the day, Shelly. In the blooming hours. I'm going to try."

ACKNOWLEDGMENTS

When darkness presses hard against us, it's easy to forget the light that burns within.

Every day, everywhere I go, I see these little lights blazing around me. I'm grateful for the kindness of strangers, for the courage of the frightened, and for the friendship of wanderers whose weird is different from mine.

Every act of compassion, every word of connection, no matter how small, reverberates beyond the stars. You may feel unseen, but you are not unfelt.

A special thank you to the Loveland Community Kitchen for giving me and anyone experiencing food insecurity a safe haven, without vetting or judgment, and for each of you, in every community, who work to build connection and combat suffering.

This book owes its breath especially to Mary Vensel White and the Type Eighteen family, who believed in this story first, and to editor Katie Schwab, who diligently dusted the dross from the gold.

ABOUT THE AUTHOR

Photo Credit: Nika Refr Wolfe

Cassondra Windwalker earned a BA of Letters from the University of Oklahoma. Born and raised on the red clay, she's wandered the sticky corn fields of the Midwest, the frozen seas of the Wild 'North, and frequently rests her wings where orange skies meet purple mountains. She's the author of novels and poetry and does her best to keep fed a menagerie of stray critters, cryptids, marooned kelpies, and lost specters.